Next Top Vampire

By Phil Sketchy

Richard and I spray painted the words, *I hope you die, President Mitchell*, on the side of the financial aid building on Washington Bay University campus, in Fort Lauderdale, Florida.

Late at night, on a Saturday, there was a full moon in a cloudless, dark blue sky. Richard and I were constantly scoping out the area, as we spray painted the message in large print on the wall. Very few people were walking anywhere near the financial aid building. Most of my colleagues were either partying at a club, in their dorm room with a significant other, or finding food and entertainment off campus.

After Richard and I finished, we took a few steps back, smiling at our artwork work. We had outlined our message in three different colors and even spray painted a stick figure stabbing another figure, labeled with President Mitchell's name. "This is beautiful. I can't wait to see President Mitchell's face when he sees this," I sighed, while turning to look at Richard.

Richard and I had been best friends since the eighth grade. Richard was a bulky, pale skinned guy. Richard was usually very quiet and rarely opened up to anyone that he didn't know. At times, Richard's presence would scare me. Sometimes when we were in my room, talking or playing video games, out of the corner of my eye, I would see him just staring at me without any expression and without saying a word. I would tense up until a goofy, childish smirk would come on his face whenever I turned to look at him. Although at times Richard would creep me out, he turned out to be the best friend a guy could have. Once when I was getting beat up by some bullies in high school, Richard came in that bathroom and beat the stuffing out of those jerks. When you stand only a couple inches over five feet and weigh about 150 pounds, soaking wet, keeping a gentle giant will help to ensure your liveliness around muscle bound freaks. Richard and I were partners in crime. We even decided to both major in Pharmacy at the same University.

Richard smiled and looked at me, "Are you ready for some abuse, man?"

"Yeah, I guess so. We're in this thing too deep now to turn back."

I grabbed the bag from where I had stashed it, in a bush before we began the spray painting.

. I took out four glass beer bottles, a blind fold, two small tissue rolls and a whip. Richard gathered some small branches from around the area. He got on his knees in front of me and I placed the blindfold over his eyes. I placed one of the small tissue rolls in his mouth as he tied the blindfold on. Richard took off his shirt and knelt with his hands under his butt. I pick up one of the branches and began to beat Richard repetitively across his back, chest, arms and legs at nearly full speed. Richard moaned and grunted as I beat him, my swings forming a figure eight pattern.

After three minutes of beating Richard, I picked up the whip and began to strike him against his back, chest and arms. He screeched when the end of the whip cut through the skin. Sometimes the whip cut through the skin so deep that it would get stuck under the first layer of skin. I had to yank the whip hard to snag it free. On the end of the leather whip, we had attached three fishing hooks and glued small pieces of colored glass that we found in an alley. Small streams of blood ran down Richard's back and his back was red all over. The blue veins in his back showed through the surface of his pale skin. I whipped Richard for only a minute to ensure that he did not lose too much blood or go into shock.

"Good job, Big Rich!" I yelled. "We're almost through, hold on!"

I picked up two of the glass bottles next to the bag and raised them above Richard's head

"Okay, on the count of three...one…two…three." I squatted down and smashed one of the bottles over Richard's head.

Richard screamed. "Oh dear God!"

I got up and slammed the other bottled over his head. "That's it Rich, you've done it, big dog. You alright, man. Can you hear me?"

Richard rolled over on his side, holding the top of his head. "Jesus. That hurt. Oh man. Mother. My Lord."

I walked over to my bag and picked up a bottle of hydrogen peroxide.

"Richard, let me see your back. Just let me clean the cuts and then it's your turn," I said, smirking.

Richard showed me his back as I opened the bottle. There were gashes all over his back, and in some areas a layer of filmy puss filled the gashes. Richard screamed violently as I poured the peroxide over his back, arms, and chest. I took off Richard's blindfold as I handed him his shirt. I put the blindfold on and got down on my knees as Richard stuffed a small tissue roll in my mouth.

Richard whispered, "I'll go a little easier on you with the strikes, since there is an obvious difference in weight." I nodded and made the okay sign with my fingers. Richard began to beat me in the same way I beat him. I was very antsy and grunting more loudly than Richard was, although he was hitting me at a quarter of the speed that I was hitting him. Jesus! Just think what I might have done if he had been hitting me at full force! I nearly passed out after the whipping and nearly fell over on my face.

Richard removed the blind fold. "Seems like you had enough. I don't think you'll make it through the bottle smashing segment. Let me clean the gashes."

"Awww! Help me. Please Jesus. Christ!" I screamed as Richard poured the rest of the hydrogen peroxide over the cuts on my chest, arms and back.

My knees wobbled as I got up on my feet. "Thanks, Richard."

I took all the supplies and placed them back in the bag. I walked over to the end of the street and stuffed the bag down a sewer drain. Richard handed me my shirt as I called the police on my cell phone.

The operator picked up. "911, what is your emergency?"

"I liked to report an assault."

"Were you assaulted, sir? Do you need medical assistance?"

"Yes, my friend Richard and I were beaten up badly."

"What is your name and location?"

"My name is Greg Rotten. We're on 314 Wanish Drive, near the financial aid building on Washington Bay campus."

"Okay sir, we are sending police and medical personnel."

"They're on their way." I grinned, looking at Richard.

"I think someone is coming," Richard muttered as we kneeled down in the grass to begin to make contorted poses.

We closed our eyes, stretched out our limbs and whined together, "Help us. Please help us. Someone."

Footsteps came near where we lay in the grass. "Wow! What happened to you guys? Are you okay?" a tall man, wearing combat boots and a backwards cap, said.

"Maybe we should call the police, Jack. Looks like they need some serious help," a blonde lady, wearing a skin tight mini skirt with a spaghetti top and high heels, said.

Once,"Help us. We need help, .please," I said as I opened my eyes and got up on one knee.

A couple stood in front of Richard and me on the sidewalk. I recognized the guy from biology class. I thought his name was Chris. I had never seen the blonde girl before.

"Greg, is that you, man? What kind of drugs did you guys do last night?" Chris said smiling.

Richard rolled over onto one knee. "A group of people. Some women and men attacked us with whips and sticks."

Chris busted out in laughter. "Dang, they beat the piss out of you guys. What did you do? Steal the beer out of their fridge? Ah ha. You losers are so weak. You couldn't even fight off a group of some old drunken buffoons. I can tell you guys don't get any booty. You…"

The girl cut Chris off. "Chris. Be nice. Cut it out. Hi, my name is Heather. Do you guy's need us to call the cops?"

"Screw that. These weirdoes look ok to me."

 "Your mother. Sissy…"

 Chris slapped Richard in the face before he could finish his sentence. Richard grabbed Chris's neck with both hands, choking him as he stood up. Heather and I both rushed over to Richard to calm things down as we heard police sirens in the distance (approaching). Richard released Chris and I pulled Richard away as the police and an ambulance pulled up. Chris and Heather walked off as a tall and skinny, white police officer got out of his vehicle. The police officer came up to me and Richard. "Which one of you is Greg?"

I raise my hand. "Me. I wanted to report an assault on me and my friend, Richard."

"How long ago did this take place?"

"An hour ago."

"Where were you guys headed?"

"We were headed to a club. You know the club Chevy's on Tenacky Street?"

"Yeah…sure. Did they take anything from you? Any personal items?"

"No. They just attacked us and left a note."

"A note. Let me see."

I handed the police officer a note that I made earlier in the day to look like an angry mob had wrote it.

Dear President Mitchell,

If you continue to cut scholarship funds from the students at Washington Bay University, we will continue to attacks several of the students on campus. We will begin with these two students as proof that we are serious about assaulting several students on campus.

Sincerely,

Your worst nightmare.

The cop shook his head. "Okay, they want to help students by making sure they get scholarship funds, but at the same time they are going to hurt those same students if their demands aren't met. Does that make sense?"

I shrugged. "That's what they said."

"Did you get a chance to look at their faces?"

"Well, it was kind of dark and I couldn't see their faces that well. It was at least ten people. Blacks and whites. Males and females. They all were in their twenties to thirties."

"What kind of clothes?"

"Dress clothes. It looked like they were coming from some kind of business meeting or something."

"Okay that's good enough. Let me get your contact information and then I want you both to get in the ambulance for medical attention."

Richard and I gave him our phone numbers and got into the ambulance. Following the treatment that we received at the hospital, upon arrival, The Hospital gave Richard and me the option to call or not call our parents because we were both eighteen years old. Of course, Richard and I refrained from calling our parents and turned down the option for the hospital to call our parents.

After spending the night in the hospital, Richard and I were swamped by reporters with questions about the incident. We told them the same story that we had told the police officer on the scene on that day, with teary eyes and lots of sobbing between questions. After receiving stitches and spending a few days in the hospital, frantically spreading false, dramatized accounts of what happened, I left the hospital feeling refreshed and confident our story would be on the news and in the mouths of everyone on campus. I could picture girls that would never take a

second look at me suddenly intrigued with my presence and hoping for any small opportunity to

express their sadness and support to Richard and I. Even guys that were tempted on a daily basis

to beat me up for looking so lame would be walking up to me to pay me some respect and

inviting me to party with them.

Two

I caught a bus to the spot on campus where I had parked my car before the hoax. I sped to

my dorm building in my red Ford Taurus and quickly ran to my small room.

I began flicking through the different news channels on the television balanced on my

dresser. "Dang. Nothing yet," I said to myself as I lay back on my twin bed against the wall and

sighed.

I ran back to my computer and began to search through several news websites. Maybe

they posted it, online. There was a quick knock on the door, before Richard walked on in

smiling. "Did they talk about us on the news?"

"No, they didn't say anything. And it just doesn't make sense. We must have talked to at

least ten reporters from different stations. And not one has reported anything on our story. They

didn't even make mention of us in the local newspaper or on any news website. Goodness

gracious! You know your existence means nothing to people when you could be brutally beaten,

nearly killed next to a school within half a mile of several news stations and get no news coverage on your story at all. Not even a sympathy call. Geez! If a better story came up. I would have at least liked to know what it was."

Richard shook his head. "Yeah. I know what you mean."

"Instead of reporting on what is really happening in our city, they want to report on what celebrity is getting married and what new cell phone is coming out in stores. What does a guy got to do to get a small dose of fame here? You remember Ashley Parker."

"Yeah, the freshman girl that transferred here from Georgetown University. She got beat up by five girls for sleeping with one of their boyfriends."

"See what I mean, man," I said, pointing at Richard.

"Yeah. That story was all over the news. She tried to sue the school and everything .she wasn't even that badly beat up. She was a pretty big girl. I guess it was big news because she used to be starting point guard for the Hoyas. What are we going to do?"

"Let's go out with some more spray paint and find some big rocks to throw."

"Uh uh. I can't take another beating for a while. I got stitches nearly going from the back of my head down to my crack."

I shook my head, "The rocks aren't for us. We're going to find some windows to throw the stones through and then we're going to spray paint the same message that we used on the financial aid building on each of our targets. Once our destructive acts have drawn up a strong spirit of outrage in this neighborhood and campus, the police and everyone in the city will be yearning for any clues on the people that have done this. That's when the police and Media will look into their past leads and our story will resurface. At that point, Richard, our names will be known all over town. Everyone will want to hear any information that we can give them about our made up mob."

"Sounds beautiful, man," Richard said, looking out the window.

I grabbed my bag of used spray paint bottles and walked out with Richard. As we headed down the hallway on the second floor of my dorm, we heard someone screaming hysterically in one of the dorm rooms ahead of us. Richard and I sprinted to the door and I began to bang on the front door. "Hey. You all right, man? Do you need some help?"

The door opened and Jeremy Winters greeted us with a stoic look. "Richard and Greg. What's up, guys? What do you want?"

Jeremy was a puny, white boy with messy, dark blond hair and cold grey eyes. Jeremy always had a nonchalant attitude about everything. Once in high school, Richard, Jeremy and I had been chased home by a pit bull.

Jeremy on our way home. Richard and I managed to get on top of a car before the pit bull could attack us. Jeremy wound up falling as we made a desperate jump on top of a car. Even as Jeremy was bitten, curled up in fetal position, I barely saw any expression cross his face. Thank God a passerby saw the dog chasing us and called animal control. A few minutes later and Jeremy would have died due to blood loss, not even trying to escape the dog's grip.

"When did you move in the dorm?" I said, grinning.

"Yesterday. I got into an argument with my roommate and had to move out."

I shook my head. "What was that noise?"

"Oh. I cut myself."

"Cooking? In the dorm?"

"No, because of stress," Jeremy said, while showing us the steak knife in his right hand and the gashes on his left forearm.

There were three parallel lines cut into Jeremy's arm. The flesh around the cuts was red. The droplets of blood that sprouted, from the pink sub layers of the epidermis, as a result of the exposure of air to the wound, sat in the pockets of the broken skin.

I shook my head and giggled. "Oh. You still into that? What a freak! You need some help man," I said, teasing.

"Yeah. Yeah. Shut up. You guys want to come in? You can sit on my bed; I got lots of beer in the mini fridge. I got this guy to buy it for me for five bucks and a free bottle/can."

"Cool." I sat with Richard on Jeremy's bed.

Jeremy sat in a folding chair and grabbed a bottle of rubbing alcohol off his desk. "So what have you guys been up to tonight?" Jeremy said, as he poured the alcohol over his injury.

I grunted, "Richard and I staged a hoax, but unfortunately, things didn't go according to plan."

Jeremy crossed his arms, "You staged a hoax? What kind of hoax? Why wasn't I invited?"

I turned and looked at Jeremy, "We didn't really know how well the hoax would work, and if it was worth dragging another person into our risky plans. Plus, we were a bit unsure if you would be game enough to partake in our scam, because you had a big exam coming up."

Jeremy smirked, "If you would have told me in advance, I could have set aside some time in my schedule to help you guys. Tell me about this hoax. What was the plan?"

I sat up in my chair, "Richard and I planned to spray paint the words, *I hope you die, President Mitchell*, on the side of the financial aid building. After spray painting the wall with an ugly message, we would brutally assault one another. All part of our scam to convince the media, the police, and everyone on campus that a mob of angry residents was planning to attack students on campus, if President Ronald Mitchell, continued to cut scholarship funds for the year.

Jeremy put gauze over the gashes in his arm, "Sounds like ya'll had fun. I'm guessing all this was for a little attention?"

I nodded, "Yes. Think about it. This deception would draw lots of attention from our colleagues and the media and we'd finally rise to fame and finally make friends with all the popular cliques on campus. We might of even gotten a couple of hot girlfriends out of all it."

"Well, what happened? How did the hoax go? Did you get caught?" Jeremy smiled.

"No, everything went according to plan, but the results weren't what we expected. The police seemed careless, the reporters seemed unimpressed and even this guy, Chris, with his girlfriend, showed a bare minimal amount of pity or concern for us lying there, bleeding in the grass. I got over fifty stitches and was bruised from head to toe, in front of a major building on a prestigious university, and not one news station, even a small time reporter working out of his basement on YouTube, even considered mentioning our story at all. Might as well been invisible. We did all this in vain," I said, almost tearing up.

"Don't talk like that, man. Who knows, maybe they still are going to cover the story. They might have had too much news to air and are saving the anecdote for later this week," said Richard.

Jeremy wrapped the gauze on his cuts, "What's up with tonight? You guys want to try a club?"

"I'm Okay, I 'm not in a club type mood right now. I don't really like the clubs too much anyway. Especially on this campus. A lot of the girls, they're are all stuck up. Won't dance with anyone unless they have some kind of status or they are extremely handsome or they are some

kind of womanizer," I said, shaking my head.

Jeremy nodded. "I know exactly what you mean."

"The club wouldn't be so bad, if I was in a better mood, and we just went to talk and have

a few drinks. Just to get out of dorm for a while," I said, unfolding my arms.

"Well, since we're not going out tonight, I got something to show you guys." Jeremy

pulled a DVD out of his drawer.

He held it up so we could read its title: *Jeffrey Dahmer: Uncovered*. "I picked it up at the

red box. It was just released. I'm surprised that all the copies weren't checked out. I would have

thought this would be a hot item. But I guess some people don't really know what a good movie

is."

I grinned. "You are awesome, Jeremy. I'm glad that you picked up a copy. I love monster

stories. Did you watch any of it? Put it in, man."

"Come on man, start it off at the beginning so Greg and I can catch up," Richard crossed

his arms.

Jeremy popped the DVD in and we watched the film from the beginning. After watching

Jeffrey Dahmer beat an 18-year-old man unconscious with a dumbbell and then strangled him

with the bar of the dumbbell, Jeremy shouted, "That shit was awesome!"

Richard clapped his hands, "When I saw him strangling that man with that bar, it gave me

an adrenaline rush."

"He must have felt powerful, bludgeoning that man with a dumbbell for angering him by

resisting his advances. I can just imagine how good it would feel to do that to someone that

enrages me like that block head, Chris. To see Chris, tied up before me, squirming to get loose and crying. Then I'd just take a bat and beat him over the head until his skull ruptures like a herpes sore. What the fuck do you got to say now, bitch!" I said, rocking back and forth in my chair.

Richard swung a make-believe bat at the floor in front of him three times. "Think you all that because you got a hot girlfriend, fuck your girlfriend, bitch!"

We all sat back in our chairs, cheering, as the movie continued. Richard whispered, "Gross!", as Jeffrey Dahmer ate a piece of a man's heart after cutting up his body and placing his decapitated head in the refrigerator.

Jeremy licked his lips. "I wonder what that would taste like."

I nodded, "looking at the way that he licked his fingers, it can't be that bad.

Richard shook his head. "I don't think I could ingest flesh, raw, with all the blood on it. I might be tempted to give it a try if it was cooked."

We all leaned forward in our seats as the movie progressed.

After we had been watching the documentary for about thirty minutes in, Jeremy stopped the DVD and looked around the room. It was as if he heard something.

"What's up, man? It was just getting good," I said scornfully.

Jeremy smiled, "I just thought of something that might change everything."

"What's wrong with you? What are talking about?" Richard frowned.

Jeremy rubbed his chin. "How many interviews has Jeffrey Dahmer done?"

"Probably over a hundred. Why?" I asked with my arms crossed.

"How much do you think the news and book writers have made off covering Jeffrey Dahmer?" Jeremy whispered.

"Probably millions. Gee, if that guy would have ever lived long enough to get out of jail. Or better yet if he had been acquitted like O.J. Simpson and wrote a book. He might be a millionaire. Look at Casey Anthony and the news stations willing to pay her tens of thousands of dollars for an interview. Jeffrey and Casey are nearly celebrities because of all the news coverage." I looked at Jeremy.

"It almost makes you think if we had committed a major crime. We might be celebrities right now." Richard said, nodding.

"Yeah. We might be. That might be exactly what we need to do." I stood up. "Don't be silly. It is not that easy to commit a Homicide and get away with it. With all the advancements in forensics, it's nearly impossible to avoid being caught. It sounds cool, but committing the perfect murder would take a lot of planning!" Richard said, chuckling.

"Think about it. O.J. was able to get off and if I remember right Jeffrey was close to getting off on an insanity plea. We just got to be smart about this. Think about all the money we would get from interviews and the ladies. Man. Haven't you heard about all the women that write to serial killers and murderers in jail?" Jeremy smiled.

"Yeah, women like them because they're dangerous. You know, it might not be such a bad idea. We'd go from losers to celebrities. We would be on television. Everyone would know our names and want our autographs." Richard hopped up on his feet.

"Well, if we're really serious we need to think this thing out. We got to worry about the police, our families, the families of the victims and we have to outshine all the other murderers in the Unites States," said Jeremy.

"Yeah, you're right. We need a set of rules—some guidelines and a plan to make this thing happen. If we can get this scheme to work, we could go from being a group of sloppy Joes to a group of legends," I said, rubbing my hands together.

Richard smiled, "What do you think they would call our clique in the newspapers? We need a catchy street name and some signature evidence that the media could identify us with. How about…..?"

Richard looked around the room and gazed upon Jeremy's shirt that had Washington Bay University imprinted on it in cursive, "The Washington Bay……. Vampires. What do you guys think of that name?"

Jeremy and I looked at each other and then back at Richard as we clapped.

Jeremy, high fived Richard, "I like it, but what sucks about all this, is that I had just gotten my silver fangs removed from my mouth, a few months before the school year started. When I was in high school, I had silver fangs put in my mouth after I had some teeth removed because of cavities. I had to beg and plead for my mother to let me get them implanted. I had to get the fangs removed during my senior year in high school so that I could get past the admission boards at a good university. If I would have kept them, it would have gone perfect with our theme. After killing our victims, I could bite them on the neck and suck some of the blood out of them."

Richard shook his head, "I already told you earlier that I can't eat anything raw, but maybe you can drink the blood for us."

Jeremy licked his lips, "well I don't have the fangs anymore, but maybe we can improvise. We could find a steak knife or something that we could use to leave puncture wounds on the neck of our victims that look like bite marks and maybe instead of drinking the blood, we could find some other way to help the media identify us as the Washington Bay Vampires.

Maybe some kind of written message."

I tapped Jeremy on the shoulder, "How about we write a scary message on the walls in blood after we finish our victims? Something like….Beware of the vampires on campus or something to that effect."

Richard and Jeremy both looked at me, nodding, "Cool!

I folded my arms, "The biggest thing will be how to avoid being convicted after we are caught. I personally think that an insanity plea will work best. If they believe that we are not sane enough to stand trial, they have to let us go or at worst send us to a mental institution for a few years. We'll just have to do our murders in such a vicious way that no one would question whether or not we are insane."

Jeremy clasped his right hand, "They say that one of the signs of a psychopath is someone that tortures and kills animals. I never really told you guys this, but…. when I was younger, my father had a drinking problem and was very physically abusive with me. At first I used to wallow in self-pity, in reaction to the abuse. As time went on and the abuse continued, I started to build up a lot of anger inside and I was looking for some way to displace my anger. One day, after my dad beat me with a toaster, I walked into the backyard, bloodied and saw some ducks walking in a pack. I picked up a brick and threw it at the ducks, knocking one of the ducks back to the ground as the others flew away. As the duck went into a convulsion, I picked it up off the ground. I carried the bird to a shed in my backyard and searched for a hammer.

By the time I found a hammer, after a few minutes of searching, the duck had died. Pretending that the duck was alive, I bludgeoned the dead duck with the hammer. As I beat the dead duck, I pretended that the dead duck was my father and I felt a rush go through his body. As a result of beating the dead duck, I didn't feel angry anymore. From that day forth, every time that I felt stressed, I would go to my backyard and catch a duck. The first few times that I beat a live duck to death, I vomited. As time went on, after killing duck after duck, my vomiting ceased and the ducks became nothing more than nail heads with feathers and beaks. After my tenth duck, the quacking as I beat them made me laugh. It wasn't until I was caught by my dad and sent to a psychologist that I gave up my hobby."

Richard shook his head, "That's awful, man! Why didn't you share something like that with us before? If you needed someone…"

Jeremy spurts out, cutting Richard off, "No! I'm not looking for sympathy. The main reason I'm sharing this with you is because it is significant in the fact that it led up to an event, where I knew I had reached a point of near insanity. When I first visited my psychologist and I explained everything to her about beating the ducks, I left out the parts about my father abusing me and instead focused on why I liked to beat the ducks. As I talked about the joy of abusing those ducks, I could see tension growing in the room between me and the Lady, Mrs. Wynn. As I continued to speak, Mrs. Wynn sweated profusely, her hands kept shaking, she never would look me in the eye and she would often slur and mumble her opinions to me. Initially upon meeting me, Mrs. Wynn had no problem articulating her thoughts to me, until after our first conversation about killing the ducks. I was crazy and Mrs. Wynn knew it. After lots of sessions and after following lots of Mrs. Wynn's suggestions, I was able to recover to a healthy mental state. The funny part about all this is that when I look back at that time when I was quote on quote, unhealthy, as one of the most enjoyable times of my life. I never felt more alive! I've been able to channel my temptation from harming ducks to self-mutilation."

I uncrossed my arms, "Don't take this the wrong way, Jeremy, but I feel you. When we were watching the scene where Jeffrey Dahmer beat that man to death with a dumbbell, it aroused me."

Richard nodded, "I thought I was the only one."

Jeremy placed his hand over his heart, "That arousal is all we need to convince a jury of our insanity. If you guys are serious about this, I can mentor both of you and teach you how to feed that excitement. When you go back to your dorms today, make a list of all the people that make or have made you angry and post it somewhere on your wall, where you will see it every day. As time progresses that arousing rage will take over you. "

Richard and I looked at each other and then at Jeremy, "We're serious!"

I steepled my fingers, "We'll be sure to complete that list when we get back. To keep our rage in order, I have a suggestion. I think that we should put together a list of rules to follow as we commit these murders to extend the length of our murder spree and to ensure that our plan flows smoothly."

Jeremy rocked back and forth in his seat, "that's not a bad idea. Let's brainstorm for an hour and write down what practices that we should follow during our terror spree. Then we'll share our rules with each other to put together a list of guidelines that we all feel are essential to the success of our scheme."

Jeremy got out of his seat and pulled some loose leaf paper out of the top drawer of his desk. Richard and I grabbed a pen from a cup full of pens sitting on Jeremy's desk. As Richard and I sat down, Jeremy handed us some paper.

After brainstorming ideas and lots of discussion, we produced seven golden rules that we would follow. First, the Washington Bay Vampires would never murder anyone we had a personal grudge against. Since most people are killed by someone they know, breaking rule number one would lead police right in our direction.

Rule number two: vampires would never brag about the murders to anyone. Word of mouth may travel to the police.

As a result, rule number three forbidded vampires from talking to police at all costs.

Rule number four: vampires would kill all witnesses on the scene. Dead witnesses don't talk to police or anyone else.

Rule number five: vampires would never kill anyone in a public place. There was bound to be a camera, a security guard or police officer, or a hero somewhere around. .

Rule number six: vampires must leave our signature on or around their victims.

Rule number seven: vampires would keep the community fearful of their existence. We would commit our crimes in such a manner that it would cause enough panic, fear and talk throughout the community that it would generate lots of buzz in the media.

In addition to following seven golden rules, we agreed to meet after each murder to put together an alibi and change our plans if things went sour. Our targets would be individuals who were infamous on campus. Killing beloved, iconic figures would cause more than uproar on campus. The killers would hunted by everyone. We'd be lucky to make into police custody alive and with all our limbs still attached. Innocent victims arouse conscience—we'd carry a lot of guilt for murdering anyone saintly or popular. If we chose individuals we, like most people, disliked, it would be easier to carry out the murders without guilt. Our hatred would fuel passionate slayings to disturb even the most hardcore students on campus. To begin our rise to fame, our first killing would have to be disturbing enough to shatter the bravest student's hope for a good night's sleep. We selected our first victim: Mrs. Sternverger, one of the financial aid workers in the President's building. Mrs. Sternverger greeted all the students with a frown. She would roll her eyes while talking to you and look away to work on her computer while you were in the middle your sentence. Sometimes she would say your scholarship check hadn't come in, when in fact it had arrived a month ago. The funny thing was, Mrs. Sternverger was the only financial aid worker known by name. All the others were "the lady with the blond curly hair" or "the man with the thick glasses and receding hairline". Mrs. Sternverger was six feet tall, at least two hundred pounds with black close trimmed hair. She had two buck teeth with one protruding out the top side of her lips. I when I met her during the first week of my freshman year. I waited in the financial aid line for about an hour, since they only had one teller. When I got up to the front of the line, she looked at me and sighed while shaking her head. I thought maybe she was thinking about something that happened earlier. I walked up to her and she said, "Excuse me boy! You need to go back and wait till you're called."

"There's no one at your counter."

Mrs. Sternverger put the palm of her hand, a few inches from my face, "Don't worry about that. You just need to follow instructions. Okay!"

"Yeah sure. Whatever," I whispered, as I stepped back.

She signaled for me to come closer. "Now, what did you come here for today?"

"I need to see if my private loan came in yet. If there is any money left over, I need it to —"

"Whoa, whoa, whoa, young man. Don't bring all that up here. I don't think you're getting any extra money, anyway. The government cut the amount of financial aid each student is supposed to get."

"I already know that. That's why I got the loan."

"Well, you don't have to be so pushy. I was just trying to help. I don't see anything on file, saying that you signed up for a loan. Here, fill out these forms and we'll know within the next two days or so if you're approved."

"Wait. My mom already filled out these forms twice. Once by mail and again online. Isn't that enough?"

"There ain't nothing wrong with doubling up on paperwork."

"Can't you just tell me if the loan came in?"

She started typing. After a minute or so she looked back to me. "My computer is moving slow right now and most of our system is down. You're going to have to come in tomorrow morning to see if your loan came in. I'm sorry, honey."

"Come on, I've been waiting in line an hour. What about these people behind me? Is the system down for them, too?"

"I'm only one person, baby. I can't work miracles. Now I will see you in the morning!"

As I walked off, my English professor, Ms. Wilson, walked past me and up to Mrs. Sternverger. "Oh, new computers! They look very expensive."

Mrs. Sternverger giggled. "They just installed them yesterday and they work beautifully. I haven't had any problems with them yet."

I shook my head and walked home to my dorm, angry and upset.

It was going to feel nice to see Mrs. Sternverger reaping what she had been sowing all these years. It probably would be best to catch Mrs. Sternverger at home, preferably when her husband was away. We would need to wait till nightfall to keep out of the neighbor's sight. Richard, Jeremy, and I wrote all our plans and rules down on paper.

"Well guys, it's getting late. It's about that time to head out, I got class at 8:15am tomorrow," I said, looking at my watch.

"I feel for you, man. That is too early. I told you should've scheduled all your classes after 11 'o clock so you can sleep late. What you got, Calculus?" Richard shook his head.

"Nope, organic chemistry. If I miss another class, Mr. Larven might drop me from his class. Dang! I figured I'd take all my classes early and get out early to have my whole afternoon to hang out before bed, but I guess it doesn't matter how I schedule my classes, I'm just a night owl," I said, smirking at Richard.

"Hey, don't forget to get Mrs. Sternverger's license plate after class tomorrow. She leaves a half hour or so after the financial aid building closes at 5. I used to see her leaving every day when I got out of my last class around that time last semester," said Jeremy.

"Why not follow her on Thursday evening, when we're all free from class?" I asked.

"Someone might see our car. I know a website that we could use to look up her address online with her license plate number. You get her license plate tomorrow and on Thursday, we'll take care of her. No leads. No suspects. No red flags. Everyone clueless about who did the murder," Jeremy said, rubbing his hands together.

Jeremy began walking backwards towards the door as he said, "Mrs. Sternverger drives a red 1992 Honda Accord with a dent in the front end of the driver's side and missing hubcaps on both rear tires. At least, if she hasn't fixed up her car since the last time I've seen it. Richard will get our outfits tomorrow and I'll scope out Mrs. Sternverger's neighborhood after I look up her address."

"Okay, cool. We'll see you tomorrow, Jeremy. Come on, Richard, let's head out," I said, heading out the door with Richard. We'd have a long day tomorrow.

Three

After my final class ended at 2pm on Wednesday, I walked over to the school library and

sat on the third floor where only a few people were studying. I stayed in the library till about

5pm, and then headed to the financial aid building.

I began to search the parking lot for a red Honda accord. The parking lot stretched around

half of the financial aid building in an L-shape with enough spaces to park 100 cars. I saw about

three red Honda Accords. One was sitting ten feet in front of the financial aid building, parked

illegally. The other two were in the same parking lot row, five cars apart. I started with the two

Accords that were sitting in the same row. I looked around the area for drivers as I walked

around both cars, looking for a dent to no avail. Maybe the Accord by the Financial Aid

building? As I began to walk toward the illegally parked car, Mrs. Sternverger exited the

financial aid building. She put a box in her back seat. She jumped in her car and speed ahead

over a speed bump. Her car landed hard and the license plate rattled loose. I was standing in the

parking lot near one of the two exits. One exit ran from the back of the financial aid building to a

busy street. The other exit ran from the area around the entrance to the financial aid building to a

residential area near campus with lots of frat houses and apartments that eventually lead to busy streets. Mrs. Sternverger got out her car to look at the back of her vehicle. She looked around the

parking lot and stared at me for a second before removing her license plate. She hopped back in

her car and drove toward me. She stopped right in front of me and rolled down her window.

"Hey, you. Come here for a sec."

"Yeah?" I said, walking towards her car.

"Do me a favor and screw my license plate back on rear of my car. Wait here, let me get

you a screwdriver." Mrs. Sternverger searched her glove compartment for a screwdriver.

She handed me her license plate and a flat head screwdriver. "Here ya go, Billy."

"It's Greg."

"Yeah. Sure. Just help me."

I knelt down behind her car. In between tapping on the rear of her car, I placed her license

plate in my book bag. I zipped up my bag and placed it on my shoulders before I got up and

walked to the driver's door. I handed Mrs. Sternverger the screwdriver and she drove off without

saying thank you and before I could sneer *you're welcome*. What a rude old hag!

#

Later that day after stopping home to eat, I walked over to Jeremy's room. "Hey bro. I got

the license plate. Open up," I said, knocking at the door.

"Cool. Come on in, let's get this thing rolling. I 'm a little anxious about how this is going

to go down. Richard called me and said he's on his way with our outfits. Hopefully he didn't pick

out something lame or cliché," Jeremy said as he ushered me inside to a chair near his bed.

"Where's your roommate?" I said looking around the room.

"Johnathan? That stupid prick left last week. I think all my talk about horror films finally

creeped him out. I tried to get him to watch a few with me, but he would always act mad uncomfortable around me. I think I was too low class for that rich prick. The guy acted like a wuss all the time. I'm glad he's gone. He snitched to the residential assistant, last week that I threaten to hurt and she moved him last week."

"Did you threaten to hurt him?"

"No. While we were playing Madden, I was slaughtering this man. I got a little too much into the game and said, 'and you thought you could beat me in Madden. I kill dudes like you in this game. Don't mess with me,' and he took that to mean that I seriously was going to try to kill him. Sissy little boy."

"Well, it can only help our insanity plea," I said, smirking.

Richard knocked at the door and Jeremy let him in.

"I got the best outfits and mask I could find for eighty bucks. Check it out!" Richard said, opening his shopping bags.

He pulled out three black nylon robes with black hoods and thin, see-through nylon fabric covering the hole for the face.

"Richard. These are perfect. I thought you were going to bring us something cheap or lame," I said, smiling.

Richard rolled his eyes. "Thanks. I'm so glad I have friends that believe in me."

Richard handed us each a pair of leather gloves. "I got these for five bucks at a second hand store. We might get lucky and have some random person's prints on them."

Jeremy sneered, "Yeah, give those cops a random point to start from."

"Okay guys, back to business. Greg gave me the license plate number. We have the gloves and outfits, and I have the weapons we need," said Jeremy as he began to search his bottom drawer.

"Greg and Richard, I got each of you one blade and one small axe, one lock pick set for each of us, and last night I took some fangs that I bought out of a hobby magazine and soldered them to pieces of wood. I call them fangers." Jeremy said as he handed us the weapons.

"Tonight, I'm going to look around Mrs. Sternverger's neighborhood for a few hours to see how often law enforcement monitors the area and how often Mrs. Sternverger's husband leaves the house. Come by tomorrow and we'll set up and plan our attack. Now go home and get some rest. It's going to be a big day tomorrow, boys," Jeremy said, grinning.

Richard and I left to get some sleep before class and before our first drop of blood on Thursday night.

#

The next day, I made my way to Jeremy's dorm room. When I got inside Richard was sitting inside playing madden on Jeremy's Xbox 360. I hopped down on Jeremy's desk seat, chuckling. "So, block heads, what's the plan? Let's get it done."

Richard said, rubbing his hands, "Well. We've decided. Around 2 a.m. tonight, we're going to take your car to an empty parking lot at a park about a half mile from Mrs. Sternverger's house. From that point, we're going to split up and head to Mrs. Sternverger's house along two different paths. This way if one or two of us are caught by police, at least one can get away. Mrs. Sternverger's house sits in the middle of a three-house block, across from three other houses. An alley splits the block in half and is used for garbage collection and also for an entrance to the garage for each house. You can see the back of every house on the block from this alley. Two of us will enter from the back and one of us will sit in front of the house as a look out until one of the others opens the front door."

"So only two of us will actually carry out the murder?" I said, running my fingers through my hair.

"Yeah. But we will change roles each time, so every one of us will eventually do a murder," Jeremy said with his hands on his hips.

Glancing from Richard to Jeremy, I said, "So who is going to be the look out?"

Jeremy tapped himself on the shoulder. "Me…but remember. If you guys can't go through with the first murder, all you got to do is gag and tie up Mrs. Sternverger and her husband and motion me in. I'll go through with it first if you don't have the heart right now. Remember, when you look at Mrs. Sternverger, look at her like she's responsible for every evil that has ever happened to you in your life."

I sighed. "Alright. Well, looks like we got it all planned out, let's get a couple hours of sleep before we head out. Let's all return back here at your dorm room, Jeremy, about 1am."

Richard and I headed out of the room. My nerves were bad and all my anxious thoughts had my palms sweaty. A little nodding off is the best remedy to calm my nerves.

#

I headed to Jeremy's house, a few minutes from the time that we decided to meet up again. We wore the same clothes we'd had on in class that day, but Richard carried a bag with our new outfits to my car. The park had a few street lights scattered two hundred feet or so apart. We parked near a dim, forest-like area. We cut eye holes in the veils, stitched them in the hoods, and put our completed costumes on. Jeremy passed around the weapons. We placed the handles of the small axes in our boots and covered the axe heads with our gowns. We placed the small pieces of wood with fangs in our shirt pockets. We carried our knives one-handed and pulled our sleeves over the hands carrying the blades as we began to exit the car. Jeremy said, "I'm going to walk back out to the entrance and walk to Mrs. Sternverger's house. You guys walk through that path that goes through the forest. That path will lead y'all to the back alley of the block that Mrs. Sternverger lives on."

 Jeremy gave us Mrs. Sternverger's address and we walked up towards her house. Richard and I made it to the alley and scanned the houses and garages on both sides. We finally reached Mrs. Sternverger's house and began to scope out the area for witnesses. The neighborhood was quiet, with the exception of a few dogs barking in the far distance and the occasional roar of a car engine on the street. All the lights were out in Mrs. Sternvergers's house including the light above her doorstep. I threw a few rocks in her yard to see if a dog would bark or coming running toward the gate. Nothing but the light sound of a bouncing rock in the grass. Richard and I looked at each other, placed hands on each other's shoulder and took a deep breath. Our first big step to a better life. Richard and I climbed over the fence slowly and began to crawl through the cut grass to Mrs. Sternverger's back porch. While we were crawling through the grass, Jeremy texted me saying, *"I'm in front of the house, Mrs. S is sleep and Mr. S is gone."*

 Richard and I crawled up the stairs of Mrs. Sternverger's porch. I looked through the partially opened blinds of the back window. I opened the screen door and Richard wiggled the doorknob to find it locked. Richard pulled up his gown to take out his lock pick set. Richard picked lock and led the way into Mrs. Sternverger's kitchen. Her sink was full of dishes, the garbage was stuffed with trash and the house smelled like cigarette smoke. There were only a few lights on above the stove and a few night lights in the living and dining room. The dining room had a few lit candles on the glass table. The living room and dining room were connected, with the kitchen counter separating the kitchen from the dining room. I tip toed through into the living room, which sat to the left of the stairs, heading for the front door. I looked through the front door peephole and saw Jeremy standing a few feet from the door with his back to the door.

I opened the lock and turned to look up the stairs. It was pitch black. Richard tip toed through the

living room behind me. Richard pulled out his silenced cell phone and pressed a number to make

the screen light up. He raised his light at the stairwell to reveal a dirty sock and a pile of

newspapers stacked on one of the stairs. Richard and I began to creep up. When Richard and I

got about halfway, we heard a low growling sound. Richard raised his phone up the stairs to

shine on a skinny Shih Tzu at the top of the stairs. Richard hid his light and the dog began to hop

down the stairs. The Shih Tzu landed right on the pile of newspapers, knocking them down the

stairs. Richard and I stiffened and looked at each other very slowly as the sound of the dragging

newspaper and the tumbling dog down the stairs died down. Richard picked up the Shih Tzu that

was now sitting on the stair behind me, sniffing my legs. Richard slowly began to walk back

down the stairs as the dog began to lick his face. I took my vibrating phone out of my pocket and

read Jeremy's text. "*What is taking you guys so long? Mr. S. will probably be back in another

10.*" Richard took the dog out to the backyard as we continued upstairs. I made it to the top

scoped out the hallway and bathroom. There were two bedrooms besides the one bathroom on

the second floor. One had the door open and the other had the door closed. I put my ear on the

closed door and heard snoring. I went into the bedroom with the open door and used my cell

phone light to look around the room. There was a desk, a bed, a lamp, two file cabinets and a

couple metal chairs. Richard's cell phone light startled me and I sighed loudly as he walked up

behind me in the room. Richard motioned me to leave and we walked to the closed door. Richard

and I began to rub our hands and wipe our faces as we slowed our breathing. We rolled up our

sleeves one-handed, while taking out our knives in our other hands. Richard pulled out his axe

from his left boot with his free hand. I grabbed the doorknob and began to slowly turn it. The door made a small creaking sound as it opened, which caused Mrs. Sternverger to stop snoring and roll over in her bed. Richard and I got down on our knees and crawled to the side of her bed where her back was exposed to us. I leaned over on the bed and held the knife within a few inches of Mrs. Sternverger's spine. I pulled my arm back a little bit and rotated my hips. I began to reflect on Mrs. Sternverger driving off without saying *thank you*, but I could not get angry enough to stab her.

After a minute or so of me standing frozen, Richard tapped me on the shoulder with the back of his fist, which held his knife. I looked at the knife and my knees buckled. Richard looked at me and giggled as he swung the axe down on Mrs. Sternverger's neck. Blood showered over me. I sighed as droplets of blood ran down my face. Richard extracted the axe from Mrs. Sternverger's spine. Mrs. Sternverger could make only a gargling sound that lasted a few seconds. I shook myself, looked at Richard with the bloody axe. Then I began to stab Mrs. Sternverger's lifeless body. I must have stabbed her at least forty times because during the last few times, the blade began entering smooth grooves made by previous cuts. Richard put his hand on my shoulder and I stopped. Unsteadily, I put my knife into its sheath on my right leg.

Richard turned on the light. "We did it."

"It's not over yet. We still have to leave our signature," I said while breathing hard.

I was drenched with sweat and my knees were shaking. There was blood all over the bed, turning the white flowers embroidered with blue flowers pink. Mrs. Sternverger's hair was drenched and blood dripped from the ends onto the wooden floor into a puddle right where I was standing.

Richard's eyes got big. "Dang it!"

"What?"

"We slit her throat. We were supposed to use the fangs on her neck to keep with our vampire theme. Now we might have to use a new name."

"Not necessarily. We can still use the fangs on her cheeks. As long as we leave fang markings somewhere, I don't think it will make a difference."

Richard and I flipped Mrs. Sternverger over on her back. She wore only a black bra and black granny panties. Blood ran from the gashes the knife had left in her chest. I took the piece of wood with the attached fangs out of my pocket and slapped Mrs. Sternverger on her left cheek with it. The fangs left two piercing holes that filled with blood. Richard stabbed Mrs. Sternverger in the stomach and began to drag the knife in a circular motion to make a large flap of skin. I grabbed the protruding flap and pulled it back to expose the intestines. I grabbed a piece of small intestine and tried to snap it off, but it only pulled more out. So I pulled all of her guts out of her stomach with both hands and cut them from her body. I then separated the large intestines from the small intestines with a knife. Richard and I began to chop up her small intestines into little pieces on the bed and toss the bits around the room. I sliced off both her ears and tossed them at the wall, leaving two bloody circular marks. Staring at them, I said, "Oh! That reminds me."

I picked up the left ear and began to drag it across the wall, painting a large letter *a* in blood on the yellow walls. Richard rubbed his chin and squinted at me as I went over to dip the ear in the pool of blood in Mrs. Sternverger's stomach. I returned to the wall with the blood drenched ear to finish my message. As I completed the first sentence, the wheels in Richard's head began to turn and he said, "Oh I see."

My message read: *all must pay tribute to the Washington Bay Vampires!*

I drew fangs on the bottom of the letters to make a vampires mouth. Next, I smeared the

rest of my message which read: *We don't want or need your money, we don't want or need your*

fame, we just want and need your blood to live!

Richard nodded his head. "Ain't that a beauty?"

I took a step back, "anything else that we should add?"

"I know what it's missing," said Richard, as he extended his hand.

I gave him the ear and Richard smudged some words under the message: See what

happens when you fuck with the wrong students on campus. You end up dead, ho.

I yelled, "Richard! What are you doing? I don't think that's such a good idea. ."

"Richard! Greg! What the heck is going on? You guys have been taking forever. Mr. S.

just pulled up. Now we've got to get him, too," Jeremy whispered, his face red and his veins

popping out his neck.

Jeremy looking around the room. "What a piece of art. Seems you guys had enough heart

to go through with it. I didn't think you had it in you."

"Richard did most of the work. I don't know if I could have done it without him," I said,

looking at the ground.

Richard shut the door and turned off the lights. Jeremy and I covered Mrs. Sternverger's

body with the bloodstained bed cover. We ran to hide in the closet. We looked through the slits in

the closet doors as we heard Mr. Sternverger walking up the stairs. "Brenda! Brenda. You still

up? I'm going to be downstairs, watching the news. I got some Burger King. I got an extra burger

if you want it. I'm going to leave it on the table."

We stood still as Mr. Sternverger headed back down stairs.

"Maybe we can leave through the window," I whispered.

Jeremy opened the closet door and we snuck to the bedroom window. It was covered with white silk curtains that had blood droplet stains all over them. We pushed back the curtains and white blinds to open the window. Outside the window was the roof over the front porch. We crawled out onto the roof and began to walk around the edges. There were bushes below the roof to the left. Parallel to the bushes was a concrete walkway separating the Sternvergers' yard from the neighboring house and leading to the backyard. We climbed the rain drain down a few feet before jumping to land in the bushes. We bruised up our legs and ripped the bottom of our gowns falling on and rolling out of the prickly branches. Jeremy reached the sidewalk and began running for our parked car. Richard and I leapt over the gated fence into the backyard. We ran through the backyard with the shih tzu barking at us and jumped over the gated fence into the alley, which we hurtled down, plunging into the woods. At last we reached the war, and waited there till Jeremy showed up and got in. We speed off into the night.

We began to breathe as I parked before our dorm, sweat pouring down our faces. You would have thought that we'd been chased by zombies if you looked at how hard our teeth were chattering. We just sat there for a few minutes without talking. Jeremy looked at his watch. "It's a little after 2am. We need to work on our timing. Everyone alright?"

Richard and I together murmured, together, "Yeah. Alright."

I turned toward Richard, "Why did you write that on the wall, Richard? Now the cops will know that some students did the murder and will come searching for us on campus."

Richard shrugged his shoulders. "I don't know. I got so caught up in paying that bitch back for all the frustration that she's caused me, that I wasn't thinking. Besides, there are over

30,000 students that attend this university and at least a third of them have had to deal with Mrs. Sternverger's dumb ass."

"Please, remember the rules in the future. Try not to do anything that connects us directly to our victim. Yes, we want to be caught, but not so soon. Give the police a bit of a challenge!" I said.

"Well, Greg, you have class in about six hours or so. Maybe, uh, you need to get a little rest."

"Yeah. Maybe so. All this excitement has got me feeling a bit drained," I slurred.

"Okay. Well, let's sleep it off and meet up after class at my place. Until then, let's all stay quiet about this. Remember tomorrow, let's go through the day like none of this ever happened. It's just a memory. If we treat it like it never happened, then eventually we will forget it and at that point in our minds, it truly never happened," Jeremy said, looking back and forth from me in the driver's seat to Richard in the seat behind me.

As Richard and I cracked open our doors, Jeremy said, "And no talking to the cops tomorrow, there are going to be a lot of cops on campus looking for leads. Remember. We're not connected to Mrs. Sternverger in anyway. It will be incredibly hard for the cops to tie us to this, unless one of us blabbed or unless someone recognized us around her house. Just stay cool and it's unlikely that they'll catch us. The only witnesses to the crime are ourselves."

Richard, Jeremy, and I got out the car and slammed our doors shut. We walked up to floor where all our dorms were and stopped a few feet before Jeremy's front door. We all took one long deep breath together, looking at one another and said, "Yeah," before heading to our rooms.

#

Four

There was lots of chatting going on in the lecture hall about Mrs. Sternverger before the

professor came. One skinny black girl tossed her long hair over her shoulder as she turned to tell

her girlfriends, "I hate to say it, but it couldn't have happen to a better person. I don't think

anybody liked that lady. I mean. Better her than me."

One of her girlfriends, a thin white girl with black hair, uncrossed her legs in her blue

jean mini skirt, "Yeah. She always had a nasty attitude. I was always nice to her. But she always

acted like such a bitch."

On my left a group of four guys whispered about the incident. One, a tall, muscular guy

with blond hair, wearing a Redskins jersey with white jeans said, "I don't know if she deserved to

be chopped up into little pieces like that. Although in the back of my mind I might of thought

about that."

Another one of the group, a black guy large enough to strain the seams of his gray suit,

moved his chair away from the tall blond guy, staring at him. "Okay. I'm going to move away

from you now. You thought about that? Weirdo!"

"Well. I mean. I'm sure every one of us at one time wanted to hurt Mrs. Sternverger for the way she treated us in the financial aid office," said the blonde guy as he looked at last the two guys in the group.

The black guy and other two shook their heads, saying together, "No. We didn't."

The blond guy shrugged. "I guess it's just me then. Sure."

Everyone got quiet as the professor came in.

Before the professor began his lesson, he walked to the front of the class. He looked down at the floor and then looked up and said, "It's a shame what happen to Mrs. Sternverger. To think that a group of people on this campus could do that to her deeply pains me."

Quiet chatter and laughter passed among the many cliques in the class of one hundred or more students. The professor looked around the class and sneered, "The Washington Bay Vampires. Hmm. I guess, eventually, you're going to get me too, huh? All the students I failed. People, we are in this all together. It is the job of every staff member on campus to do what is best for the students. I am not the enemy. Mrs. Sternverger was not the enemy. What is happening to our campus when the value of life means nothing? …I'm going to stop preaching now."

As the professor went to the board to start the lesson, Mrs. Stevens from the library came into the class, walked up to the professor, and whispered something before leaving. The professor shook his head. He turned away from the board and announced "All classes are dismissed for the day. We'll start again on Monday at 8am sharp. Don't be late."

My classmates and I left the classroom, and I began walking toward the set. The set was an area in the middle of campus near the all-female dorms, the school gym, the school post office, and lots of small administrative buildings. The offices sat next to one another in a straight line, while the nine female dorms formed a block across a long street that stretched from residential areas to the east and west of campus. Only buses designated to usher students around the campus drove through the set. Lots of small trees and plants grew along the walkways near the dorms and other buildings. On the walkway, near the school related buildings, students gathered selling art, t-shirts, cd's, DVD's, snacks and anything else a college student could purchase within their budget. After and between classes every day, students went to the set for small talk and to find out about events that were happening on campus. Many of their cliques sat down on the long concrete benches connected to the short brick walls surrounding the trees and plants. In the near distance, a blonde haired, news reporter interviewed my chemistry professor, in front of an administrative building, near the vending walkway. My chemistry professor frowned and shook his head as he answered the reporter's questions. Other students were reading the local newspaper while sitting on the benches. I glanced at the front cover as a colleague slowly walked by me. *Washington Bay Vampires Prey on Town*. I walked over to a free newspaper bin next to the school post office and picked up a copy, then sat on an empty bench to read the article. A white guy with a red shirt and a Asian guy in a suit sat down on the bench close to me and began to talk about a club they had went to last night. As the two men were talking, the white guy glanced over at the paper I was reading. "Kind of cool .huh? I mean, I feel like I'm in a horror movie with everyone so tense and all this news coverage on campus. Feels like I'm part of something big, you know?"

I smiled. "Yeah. I guess our college will get a little bit more fame especially if the murders continue. Our campus will be talked about all over the globe. Think about all the stories that we will all be able to tell after all this is over. And can you imagine the books and movies they'll make?"

The white guy nodded. "Wow! I never thought about it like that. Maybe someone will sell t-shirts with a logo that reads: Washington Bay Vampires. I mean, I would buy one. It would be nice to have some kind of memorabilia."

I nodded. "That's not a bad idea."

I folded up my newspaper and put it in my book bag. I walked over to a vendor who was selling white t-shirts at a price of five for fifteen dollars and bought twenty t-shirts. Then I crept over to the side of the financial aid building where Richard and I had spray painted our message. I surveyed the area and when the coast was clear, I began to search for any spray paint canisters Richard and I had forgotten. After searching through the sewer drain where Richard and I had disposed of our bag, I found it and pulled it out. It was covered in mold ants. I brushed off the bugs and looked inside for any canisters with paint still in them. I found two that were nearly full and placed them in my book bag. I zipped up the moldy bag and tossed it back down the drain. I found a big dumpster near the financial aid building filled with cardboard boxes. I pulled out a three by three foot box, laid it down in the grass near the dumpster and took the white t-shirts out of my bag. I put the t-shirts on the box one after another and spray painted several different slogans: "Who needs Mrs. Sternverger," "Better Financial Aid Reps.," "W.V.P.'s for life," and "I am a Washington Bay Vampire."

I waited about ten minutes for the t-shirts to dry and then returned to the set with the t-shirts in my bag. I put on one that read "I am a Washington Bay Vampire" and began to yell, "Washington Bay Vampire t-shirts for five dollars! Only five blood sucking dollars for a Washington Bay Vampires t-shirt!" \

I got various responses from people who passed by as I tried to sell the t-shirts. Some people looked at me, shaking their heads with a frown and mumbling comments from "You should be ashamed" to "insensitive prick" to "I hope they kill you next."

Other people looked at me, shaking their heads with a smile and, between chuckling, offered comments like "I wish I had thought of that" and "nice shirt."

Overall, my idea seemed to be working and I sold ten t-shirts in a half hour. In the middle of a sale, I saw Jeremy approaching with his jaw dropped. He grabbed my right arm. "Are you crazy? Don't you see all these reporters on campus?"

I took the five dollars from my customer with my left hand I turned to Jeremy as my customer walked off "What's the problem, man? Look, people are talking about our crime all over campus and I made fifty dollars in thirty minutes. And after everyone on campus buys one of these shirts, the Washington Bay Vampires will be known all over town."

"You idiot," Jeremy screamed. "You don't think the cops... We 'll talk about this at the meeting tonight. For now, get rid of those shirts. *Now*."

"Alright. Alright. Calm down. I'll get rid of the shirts. Don't see anything wrong with increasing awareness and making a little money off our work at the same time. Look at it this way, with the money that we make off these t-shirts, we'll be able to live better than any regular college students. No more peanut butter and jelly sandwiches or microwavable noodles."

"Just get rid of the shirts," Jeremy vented.

I threw the remaining t-shirts in the trash and headed for my dorm, Jeremy at my side.

#

When I entered Jeremy's room for our meeting that evening, Richard was watching The Texas Chainsaw Massacre. I sat down. "So how did everyone's day go? Did anyone talk to any reporters?"

Richard and Jeremy both said, "Naw," at the same time.

Richard vented, "Jeremy told me you were selling t-shirts on the set that said *I am a Washington Bay Vampire*."

I looked at Richard. "So? I just figured it would help spread our name on campus and besides, riches are a part of why we decided to do this is the first place. Right? If we can make a little money here and there off our work, what's the problem?"

Jeremy held his hand up at me. "Greg! We just murdered a woman and you're basically wearing a shirt that says you did. There were cops all over campus asking questions. I'm surprised those shirts didn't stir up a red flag."

I opened my arms. "Think of all the stores that sell shirts with crazy logos. I had at least ten people buy one of those shirts and no one was ever so creeped out by my presence that they didn't make a comment when they walked by."

Richard shook his head. "Be careful man. Remember, if we're trying to be as big as Jeffrey Dahmer than we have to think about our reign of terror from a long term point of view. If you keep pulling stunts like this than our killing spree will be over before we become national news. All it takes is one person to say that there was something suspicious about you."

I held up my hands. "Okay. I guess I can put aside the money I can make now for the big money I can make later. So how does everyone feel about last night? Lose any sleep over it?"

Jeremy and Richard both shook their heads and said together, "Not really."

"Well. I did lose a little sleep over it. I mean not so much because of Mrs. Sternverger, but mainly because if Richard wasn't with me last night, I don't think I could have gone through with it. I…just couldn't get angry enough to hurt her."

Jeremy said, "Just give it time. Maybe on the next one, you'll be able to. At least you were able to follow through with dismembering the body. It takes a strong mind to do something like that. My nerves got to me a bit last night, too, but I kept my mind on how much of an old hag Mrs. Sternverger always was. Stupid tramp got what she deserved. Good riddance."

Richard nodded. "Yeah, forget that dumb witch. I was little nervous, too, but something went off inside me when I picked up that axe. I just felt powerful. I felt like I was finally in control of how things work in this world. Like I had a person's fate in the palm of my hand. And I think that first strike to Mrs. Sternverger's neck and that banshee wail she let out will stay with me the rest of my life. It sends shivers up my back just thinking about it, but I guess in time, I'll get over it. I hope. I mean, there's no turning back now."

I nodded. "Yeah. So who's the next target? Is everyone ready for round two? Killing Mrs. Sternverger introduced us and brought a lot of media attention to our campus, but now it's time for us to really engrain The Washington Bay Vampires in national headlines and draw reporters from all over the country."

Jeremy said, "That's exactly it. Remember our seven rules of conduct. One of the most important is no talking to police and no bragging about the murders. *Greg,*" he added, with a stern look at me. "Our name has only scratched the surface of everyone's mind on campus, but after a few more murders, we should be on the minds of everyone in this city. I know just the right people we need to slay to build fear in the hearts of everyone in this country. At the top of that list is our starting quarterback, Melvin Peters."

I shook my head. "Melvin Peters is a big guy. I don't think one or two of us are going to be able to get close enough to stab him."

"I know. He's probably been taking steroids since the first grade," Richard said, wiping his forehead.

Jeremy smirked. "The guy's not the incredible hulk. If we pepper spray him and use a bat or a crowbar, he should be no problem."

I crossed my arms, "Well, how can get him alone? The guy is always surrounded by friends. He's a money tree and a chick magnet."

Jeremy smiled. "Exactly. We lure him to a room, thinking that he'll meet some hot broad and as soon as he enters, we hit him over the head with a tire iron."

Richard and I looked at each other and then said together, "Yeah, fucking right!"

I shook my head. "That'll never work. Where do you think you'll find a secluded room and on top of that, a secluded room Melvin Peters will just walk on into? Maybe we need to catch him at a club and put something in his drink."

Jeremy and Richard looked at each other and then said together, smirking, "Yeah, fucking right!"

"Wait a sec," Richard said. "My cousin is the resident assistant at one of the female dorms. We could find out from her if there are any empty rooms. We could trick Melvin into thinking that a girl is waiting for him there and as soon as he enters, hit him over his head."

Jeremy and I looked at each other and then back to Richard. "Yes!"

I leaned over the bed to give Richard a high five. "My man. That's perfect! All we got to do is set up a fake Facebook account with a sexy pic and lure him. The biggest problem will be finding and getting into an empty room... Richard, if you ask your cousin about empty rooms it might make her suspicious after someone dies in a room you asked about. It would connect us to the crime. We have to find a way that won't raise any red flags."

Richard said, "We could split up in the female dorm and knock on each door and see if anyone answers. If no one answers, we could pick the lock and see if the room is empty. We need to do it tonight though. If we wait till tomorrow, we run the risk of picking the doors of people who are out partying. If someone were to see us picking the lock of their friend's door, they might think we're burglars."

Jeremy looking at his watch. "It's almost midnight. Let's go before it's too late. Most people will be asleep in an hour. Wouldn't want to pick the lock of a room with the resident sleeping inside. Matter of fact, Greg, how about you and Richard go and find an empty room inside one of the female dorms and I'll set up the fake Facebook account. I'll find some pictures to send Melvin. If this guy is as whipped for women as we think, a few messages with some sexy pics and an invite should be enough to bring him in. As soon as you guys bring me back a room number I'll invite him to meet Brenda tomorrow. Our homecoming game is this Saturday. I'm sure he will want to relieve some stress before the big game. What better way than a little booty?"

Jeremy opened his drawer and pulled out a small plastic bag. He offered it to Richard and I, and I saw it held two small lock pick sets and two extension cords. We opened the bag and we each put one lock pick set and one extension cord in our pockets.

"You shouldn't have to worry much about being spotted," Jeremy told us. "The good thing about pulling this off during homecoming week is that most people will be out partying late every night this week. Not many people will be in their rooms till the clubs close."

Richard and I left Jeremy's room and headed out the dorm to the set. Standing on the set across the street from the dorms, we scanned the area. Most of the dorms farthest from us were well lit and had lots of people outside at picnic tables on the lawn. The two dorms, Forb and Sandal Foot, sat closest to us/ Tall trees growing in front of them blocked the street lights from illuminating the walkway to the front door of Forb. The walkway lights on the side of Sandal Foot, the dorm that sat closest to us on the right, were broken. We walked to the side door on the right. The right side of Sandal Foot faced a metal fence that enclosed both dorms, with about thirty feet of clear ground in between. . The only light shed on the walkway came from the half full moon. Richard and I scoped out the area as we walked up to the side door. Richard began to pick the lock as I looked through the window on the door. The hallway lights were on bright. Richard picked the lock and we walked inside. There were a set of stairs to our right. Richard turned to walk up the stairs but I grabbed his arm before he could make his first step. "I just thought of a plan. Follow my lead."

There were at least twenty rooms on the first floor, lining the hall all the way to a visitor's lounge where the resident assistant was located. I pulled my pen out and walked to the first door on my left. I knocked three times and a skinny blonde girl opened the door. "Yes?"

"Is Mary here?"

The blonde girl shut the door in my face. Nasty heifer! I used my pen to lightly scratch a line on the door under the peephole. I turned to the door behind us and knocked again. A black girl with braids opened the door. "What do you want?"

I smiled, "Is Mary here?"

The black girl shook her head. "Mary left with Terry to go to the club."

I cleared my throat and said, "Mary Peters. Right?"

"No, Mary Parker. You got the wrong door."

I said, "Mary Peters is my cousin. She just moved in this dorm yesterday. She told me she had a room on the right side of the first floor. Have you seen her?"

"Sorry, never heard of her." As she was about to close the door, I stuck my foot in the frame.

"Please ma'am, wait. I have to give my cousin money for her books tonight, because I'm transferring and leaving Washington Bay on Monday. She told me she left her door open for me to leave the money, but I'm not sure which it is. I'll figure it out on my own. But I don't want open the wrong door. Someone might think I was trying to break into their room. You seem like a really friendly person, so I'm sure you know most of the people on this floor. Do you know which rooms on this side have someone living in them? Please, my cousin really needs this money."

Richard pulled out a twenty dollar bill and gave it to the girl. She grabbed the bill and walked out in the hallway in her pajamas. She pointed at each door and told us who lived in each and which rooms were vacant. I bowed my head to the girl. "Thank you.....What's your name?"

The girl smiled, "Linda."

"My cousin will be so happy I dropped off her book money before I left," I said, as I grinned.

The girl waved bye and shut her door. I scratched an x with pen on each of the vacant doors, walked back to the first and knocked three times. There was no answer. Richard began to pick the lock and I stood on his right side to block the view from anyone that came down the central walkway. A girl came down the hall towards us with her face to the ground. I tapped Richard on his shoulder and Richard opened the door as soon as the girl. Our eyes locked and all my muscles went tight. The girl squinted at me just as Richard pulled me by my arm into the room and shut the door behind me. I wiped my face. "That was close. Do you think she'll remember us?"

Richard said, "No. It's not that unusual for guy to enter a girl's dorm room late at night. You're just a little paranoid. Besides, we haven't done anything wrong. Except break into a vacant room. The most that might happen is that she'll call the resident assistant. Hopefully she won't do either, but I don't plan staying here that long anyway."

Richard walked over to the window, unlocked it and cracked it open. I looked out the window at the buildings across the street. I took a black extension cord out of my pocket and hung the socket end out of the window so that it dangled against the outside brick wall. I tied the other end to one of the legs of the bed. Richard and I walked back out into the hallway and I wrote the room number on my hand with the pen. Richard and I left Sandal Foot through the same side door that we entered through and headed back to Jeremy's room. Jeremy let us in ushered us to two folding chairs that he had unfolded for us, before he opened the door. His open laptop showed how Jeremy was instant messaging Melvin with a fake profile on Facebook. I chuckled. "Cool. So, what does he think of Brenda? Is he ready to meet up with her?"

Jeremy smiled. "Oh, yeah. Let me show you some of the stuff he's been messaging me."

Jeremy scrolled up through his messages and pointed at one of Melvin's replies. "Right here I messaged him that I thought he was hot and would he been down to do some role playing with me in my room? Look at what he said: *Yes, Baby, we can play doctor, we can play teacher. Whatever you like, just give me the room number and time*."

Jeremy laughed. "He's totally into Brenda. That whipped meathead!"

I smirked. "Cool. We found a vacant room, 115 on the first floor of Sandal Foot dorm. Invite him."

I looked over at Richard and then back at Jeremy. "What do you guys think about tomorrow night? Is it too soon? You guys ready to take care of our next victim?"

Richard and Jeremy both nodded and Richard said, "Let's go!"

Jeremy began typing on his computer. "Alright. Let me send Melvin an invite for tomorrow."

Jeremy hit the enter key, but then grunted. "Dang. He's offline now. I must have taken too long to respond. I'll send him an email, he should read it by tomorrow. Let's get some sleep for class, I'll give you guys a call when he responds. Hopefully he'll respond soon, so don't make any plans."

Richard and I gave Jeremy some dap and left.

#

Five

Around 6pm the next day, Jeremy called me on my cell. "Melvin got back to me about an hour ago. I told him to meet me at room 116 at Sandal Foot at 1am tonight. So meet me at my place around 11pm tonight so we can plan this out. I'm going to call Richard now, so I'll see you then."

I hung up and spent the next few hours doing homework before heading to Jeremy's place. When I entered the room, Jeremy was showing Richard a Taser. Jeremy grinned, "Greg, what do you think of my Taser X26? It can shoot a target up to fifteen feet away, it only takes two seconds to reload, and although it only weighs seven ounces, it's packing fifty thousand volts, man."

I smiled. "What a cool toy. You plan on using that on Melvin? Not bad idea. One of you hop out of the closet behind the door and taser Melvin as soon as he comes in. I'll hop out from under the bed with a knife and cut Melvin open from throat all the way down to his belly button."

Jeremy squinted at me. "No. The plan was I hide under the covers with the Taser and when Melvin comes in and pulls the covers off of me, I get him. Then the two of you hop out of the closet and chop his muscle bound head off with an axe, but… I'm starting to like your plan better. Richard and I were just talking about how risky it would be for me to be under the covers. Melvin could hop on me, pinning my arms down and brutally attack me before you guys have a chance to come from the closet. Now that I think about it, trying to gut him could be risky, too, especially with an axe. If the axe is too blunt it may take time to kill him and we will have to fight this big monkey prick until he passes out. This could be several minutes. Not to mention if the neighbors hear him scream… Let me see in my drawer…..We could use the knives that we used on Mrs. Sternverger. The knives seemed sufficient …Maybe I'll bring the knives along with the axe."

Richard said, "We could sharpen the axe."

Jeremy shook his head while looking at the weapons in his drawer. "Where could we? And even if we did find a place, it would be too late now."

Jeremy suddenly looked up at me, grinning, "Oh, I almost forgot!"

He pulled out a twelve inch machete from his drawer. "I bought this about six months ago at a knife shop. This is perfect for job. Not too long. Not too short. Not too heavy. Not too light. Sharp blade, should make a clean cut through the neck and spinal cord."

Jeremy pulled out his wooden chair from his desk and slung the blade of the machete across through the back. One of the beams was cut in two and the other was cracked while the machete sat stuck halfway through the back support. Jeremy wiggled the machete free and handed it to me. "You take it. Richard and I will wait in the closet to taser him. As soon as we hop out and get him, that's when you come from under the bed with the machete. Richard will support you by gutting him with one of the knives from the Mrs. Sternverger Murder."

Richard placed his hand on my shoulder. "I believe tonight is the night for you. Last time you were a little hesitant. But that's okay. You still have a lot of innocence. It just shows that you're a sane person. While you're under the bed, just look at Melvin like he's one of the bullies that use to pick on you in high school. It'll make it easier. We all looked at the clock; it was about twenty minutes to midnight. Richard, Jeremy, and I played Madden on his Xbox 360 until then. Jeremy cut off the system in the middle of a game between Richard and me. "Let's get head out."

We left Jeremy's room with costumes and weapons in Jeremy's book bag and headed to Sandal Foot. We stopped once we reached the set and checked out the area. All the windows had closed blinds in, blocking the view of the dorms inside. We walked to the lightless right side of Sandal Foot and began to creep along the brick wall of the dorm, behind the bushes that grew before them and under their branches and the windows. We stopped at the extension cord hanging down over the window seal. I slowly rose up to check for people. After a few potential witnesses walked past the scene, I stood up completely. I opened the window and Richard and Jeremy lifted me up. I rolled over on the floor, opened the blinds, and got up to help pull Jeremy in. Richard Lifted Jeremy, as I pulled him through the window. Jeremy and I began to pull Richard in through the window, which was a struggle. Richard had to weigh at least two hundred something pounds. Maybe he should have gone in first!

After a few minutes of struggling and straining, Jeremy pushing and I pulling Richard finally got inside. He leaned over the window seal and pulled Jeremy through. Jeremy shut the window and pulled down the blinds. Then he took a white bed sheet and blue comforter from his book bag and laid them on the mattress in the room.

I watched with wide eyes. "I hope that's not your personal bed sheets. You probably got DNA all over it."

Jeremy said, "No, of course not. Look at me, Greg. All I do is watch horror flicks and cop shows. I got these sheets earlier today at a second hand store. They've got someone else's DNA all over these sheets. Now help me put the comforter over the bed."

Richard, Jeremy, and I fixed the bed, put on our costumes, and took a deep breath together. I looked at the time on my watch. It was ten minutes until 1. "You should text him to make sure that he's still coming."

Jeremy lifted the bottom of his gown to pull out his cell phone. While Jeremy was in the middle of texting Melvin, Melvin called. Richard said, "Don't answer it! Let it go to voice mail."

Jeremy had already hit *answer,* but he hung up, muttering, "No. he'll hear my voice on the answering machine. I'll text him back. I'll tell him I don't have any minutes left on my phone."

Jeremy texted him back and a couple minutes later, Melvin said that he would be at the dorm room in about ten minutes. Jeremy looked at Richard and I. "I told him that I was about to take a shower, but the door would be open. He should wait in the room if he didn't see me, and I would probably be back in a few minutes. Now, let's get to our places. Greg, remember, as soon as he enters the door I'm going to jump out with the Taser. That's when you come from under the bed and split him with the machete. We got to do this fast, no more than five minutes tops. Let's get it done and head out."

I hid under the bed and Richard and Jeremy hid in the closet. My eyes were slightly shut and I was breathing slowly while. Goose bumps sprouted all over my neck and the muscles in my arms and legs were twitching. I held my breath as someone knocked at the door twice. I heard the door creak open and saw someone in blue jeans take two steps towards the bed. I exhaled as the door slammed close and Richard and Jeremy jumped out of the closet. The next thing I heard was a high pitched scream. It died out under the electrical charge coming from the Taser. I hopped out from under the bed to see a black girl with braids fall to the floor as Jeremy let go of the trigger. I looked down at the girl vibrating on the floor, and raised the machete above her head. I remembered this one bully from high school, who used to punch me in the back every day when he would see me at my locker in the morning. My breathing deepened and my fist clenched tight around the machete. I look at Jeremy, who nodded, and when I look back at the girl, I recognize her as the one who helped me find the vacant room.

Thinking of how kind she'd been, I started to lower the machete. I'd dealt with a lot of rude women in my life and whenever I met one who was soft spoken and polite, it was a breath of fresh air. I dropped my head and turned towards Jeremy. Jeremy extended his hand for the machete and I handed it to him. Jeremy immediately slammed the machete down on the girl's neck, kneeling at the same time to put more power into his strike. Linda's head came almost completely off, held onto the body only by a thin piece of the spinal cord. The blade broke off after slicing through most of the cord and clattered onto the floor. Blood fountained from the girl's neck, forming a large puddle around her head as I blinked. Jeremy dropped the machete handle and put his hand on my shoulder. "It's alright. Just help us leave our signature."

I took out the fanger and slapped the girl on the cheek and on the thin, uncut remaining skin that held the head onto the body. I locked the door, took the knife, flipped Linda over and split open her stomach. Suddenly, someone else knocked at the door. Richard, Jeremy and I looked at each other with our eyes wide. Jeremy pointed at me and then under the bed, then went back to the closet with his taser in hand. Richard and I flipped the girl over, took the comforter off the bed, and cover her up to the back of her head, concealing the blood and the gash in her neck. I slid back under the bed and Richard returned to the closet. Melvin knocked again.

"Brenda. It's Melvin. The door is locked. You still want to see me tonight?"

Richard reached out of the closet to unlock the door and open it an inch. Melvin slowly

pushed the door the rest of the way and walked into the room, "Brenda? Where'd you go? Under

the covers already, I see. Why don't we take it on the bed first?"

Jeremy jumped out of the closet and shot Melvin with the Taser, while Richard shut and

locked the door. Melvin wailed loudly and began to move towards Richard and Jeremy with his

right fist raised and clenched. Richard ran up to Melvin, bobbing and weaving, and with quick

flashes of his knife stabbed Melvin multiple times. I slid from under the bed and sank my

machete in Melvin's back till he fell on his knees and then to the floor. Jeremy whispered sternly,

"We got hurry up and get out of here, man. I'm sure someone next door heard him wailing."

I flipped Melvin over and split open his stomach. I pulled out his guts and cut them from

his body. Richard took out his fanger and slapped Melvin across the cheek. Richard and I pulled

Melvin towards the window and took the comforter off the black girl. I pulled her intestines out.

"Help me cut this up, Jeremy."

Jeremy knelt and cut off the black girl's right ear. "Let me write our message. I'd say that

we got no more than a few minutes before someone comes, asking if we need help, or the police

respond to a phone call about a scream coming from this room."

Jeremy dipped the ear in the pool of blood around Linda's neck and began to write the

same message that I had written on the wall after we had killed Mrs. Sternverger. Richard was

quickly chopping up Melvin's intestines as I chopped the girl's. Richard and I tossed pieces

around the room. Someone began knocking. "Do you need any help? Do you need me to call

anyone?"

Jeremy pointed at me and Richard and then the window. Richard and I walked over to the window as the girl at the door knocked a couple more times. "I'm going to get some help, I'm going to get the RA downstairs."

Richard opened the blinds and scoped out the area. No one was around outside. Richard pulled the blinds up halfway and opened the window. Jeremy turned the lights off. "Careful. There could be someone, outside, looking at us."

Richard climbed out of and I followed him. We crawled alongside the brick wall behind the bushes until we reached the corner of the building. We heard a loud thud behind us and turned to see Jeremy had just landed on his feet. He began crawling towards us. Richard and I pulled the hooded, bloody gowns off and balled them up in our hands. We waited until Jeremy reached the side of the building, carrying his book bag. Jeremy, Richard and I placed our gowns in the bag and ran across the street to the other side of the set. As we cut between two buildings on the set to head to our dorm, we heard loud screams coming from the direction of Sandal Foot. Our pace sped up. As we were walking through a large field of grass near the male dorms, we spotted a garbage bag full of dress clothes sitting next to a dumpster, a hundred feet or so from the dorm named Paddy Foot. A few dress shirts and slacks had spilled on the ground around the bag.

I said to myself, "I wonder whose clothes those are?"

I visualized myself going door to door asking people whose clothes were sitting next to a dumpster. I shook my head and regained my focus. "Jeremy. I think we need a good place to get rid of those bloody clothes."

Jeremy squinted. "I'll wash them early in the morning, while everyone is sleeping, so we can use them again."

Richard looked at Jeremy. "I don't think that will get rid of all the blood. We need to burn them."

Jeremy shook his head. "Then we will have to buy another new set of costumes. I don't have that kind of money."

I said, "Well, let's at least find a place to stash the clothes. How about behind the bushes along the back of Paddy Foot?"

I grabbed the bag from near the dumpster and poured the dress clothes out on the floor. I handed the empty bag to Jeremy and he filled it with the bloody gowns out of his book bag. Jeremy tied up the garbage bag and we walked along the back of Paddy Foot until we saw a dorm room on the first floor that had the curtain closed and the lights out. We placed the garbage bag behind the bush under the lightless dorm room. We began to walk back around Paddy Foot to the front and then headed to our dorm. When we got to our dorm Jeremy murmured, "Let's sleep it off and meet up at my place whenever you guys get up tomorrow. But no later than 3pm."

I whispered, "Sure" and Richard mumbled, "Yeah."

#

That night I could hardly sleep. Sirens were constantly going off throughout the night and images of the innocent black girl that we killed keep flashing in my head. Did we really have to kill her?

Yes, we did. There really was no other way to deal with her once she entered the room and saw us with our weapons. But we could have possibly tied her up. Maybe, we could have found somewhere to hide her till all this was over. She would have made a very emotional testimony against us in court and a great chapter in one of our confessional books.

I guessed there was no need to cry over spilled milk. Hopefully, I wouldn't have to kill any more innocent people for our plans. I finally fell asleep and little after I got up the next day, I made my way to Jeremy's room. Richard was already sitting on his bed watching the news on television. I sat down next to him. "What's the word, how we looking on television?"

Richard was locked into the screen. "Better than expected. Every channel is covering the double murder in the Sandal Foot dorm. They're talking about sending the F.B.I. onto our campus to investigate. This thing is getting bigger and bigger. Melvin's status really caused the story to sky rocket."

Jeremy said, "The story is posted on Yahoo. Millions all over the country probably know about the killings and the Washington Bay Vampires. I check the T.V. Guide online, and the History Channel is doing a special on the culture of vampirism on Wednesday. We got our fifteen minutes of fame, man. Now, if we can extend our reign of terror a little longer and add to our body count, we might get bigger than Jeffrey Dahmer. Bigger than Charles Manson. We'd make Freddy Kruger look like Mr. Rogers."

I squinted. "What do you mean, man? All we gotta do now is kill or try to kill one more person and get caught during the act, fool the jury and write our books. We'll be rich, man. We'll be celebrities. How many more people do we need to kill?"

Jeremy shook his head. "You're thinking small time. So we killed two people and a financial aid worker. Some serial killers have killed over twenty people. Most of them innocent and at random."

I frowned. "I'm not killing anymore innocent people."

Richard and Jeremy both looked at me at the same time and said, "What?"

I sighed. "Did we really have to kill that girl? She wasn't even our target. She was a sweetheart. We could have let her go."

Jeremy's eyes got wide. "Are you serious? What's our rule? *No witnesses*, remember? We're too far in this thing to stop now. I'm not about to ruin all the work that I put in because your conscience is bothering you. Forget the girl. Forget her. She's water under the bridge now. Remember how we've been treated since we came on this campus? No girlfriends. The girls at the club are all stuck up. When is the last time one of the jocks or any other guys from your classes invited you to go out and party with them? Never. We're a joke on campus. The only thing that these people care about is what you can do for them. We're broke and unpopular. What can we offer them? Nothing. This thing that we have going right now, Greg, is our highway to fame, fortune, and women. And you want to give it up for some stupid broad who probably thought that we were the creepiest guys on campus. Forget her. When this thing boils over and we're identified, our faces will be on every news channel. Girls will write to us and if they don't, we'll make so much money from our books sales that we could buy affection from any girl."

I began rubbing my hands together. "I guess you're right. I didn't think about it that way. I just don't have the heart like you, Jeremy."

Jeremy placed his hand on my shoulder. "But you will. Soon, during our next murder, you'll cast the first strike. Mrs. Sternverger's death started our hype and the death of Melvin Peters is our foundation. The guy is an icon. Think about how many NFL teams were looking at him and all the attention coming from all over the United States that he was getting. The fame he had is transferred to us now. We are the center of attention."

I nodded. "It's awesome. So how many more bodies are we talking about?"

Jeremy stood up and smiled. "Remember, we're not playing a numbers game. Serial killings have probably been going on for thousands of years. Why do people like Jack the Ripper and Jeffrey Dahmer stand out of all of the killers?"

Richard said, "Jack the Ripper was one of the best known, serial killers of his time and Jeffrey Dahmer ate people."

Jeremy nodded and smiled. "Yes, but what scares people most is that Jack the Ripper was never caught, meaning that there is always that thought that he could kill you and get away with it. Same with Jeffrey Dahmer. Most people would have never guessed that he was a serial killer, if he had never got caught. In fact, one of Jeffrey Dahmer's victims almost escaped, but the police returned him to Jeffrey, because they thought they'd just had a lover's spat. It's the thought that you never know who a killer is and at anytime and anywhere, you might end up a victim by a killer like Jeffrey Dahmer and they may never catch him or her. It's a scary thought that most don't like to deal with. So it's the almost mocking evasiveness of these killers that really haunt people. We must do the same. If we kill at least a few more high profile people and get away with it, we show the police and society we can kill anyone, anytime, anywhere, and it doesn't matter how high profiled or protected. We'll find a way to get them and there is no safe place to hide. And nowhere to run. Everyone is prey. After we engrain this in everyone on this campus, the stories about our reign of terror will last forever."

Richard nodded. "So who do we need to kill to engrain that kind of fear in people?"

Jeremy sat down. "That's the dilemma. We need to think."

There was a lot of noise coming from outside of Jeremy's window. I got up and peeked through the blinds. There was a group of guys in Washington Bay football jerseys standing around a green corvette, talking loudly. Each guy's jersey had Melvin's number, 27. I turned to

Jeremy and Richard, still watching the news coverage, and then back at the guys outside. Dang, Melvin was legendary. I'm sure that at some time during this year at school, everyone was envious of Melvin. Just imagine being the star quarterback, the world is handed to you and every day is a party. I turned to Jeremy. "I know who we should kill."

Richard smirked. "Who?"

I said, "The death of Melvin caused all this news coverage because of his status as a star quarterback."

"So?"

"So, everyone was envious. Everyone must have imagined what it would be like to be him. So he was always on our minds. Now his death is stirring up all this guilt in everyone for being so jealous of him. We need to kill people who representation lifestyles we have wanted. We all at one time wanted to be a quarterback, so we did well in killing Melvin during Homecoming week, but what does every girl on campus want to be? Ms. Washington Bay for Homecoming, right? The way I see it now, if we kill off the top five people on campus, our impact on the minds of the people on campus would outweigh any number of other murders we commit could."

Richard squinted at me. "Why the top five people and not the top ten?"

"With the F.B.I. involved now and with this much coverage, I figure it's only a matter of time before the police find us."

Jeremy said, "Forensics is tough to beat. I wonder how much trace evidence the police have on us already?"

Richard said, "So who do you think are the five people that we need to take out?"

I sat down. "We already took out one, Melvin Peters. This leaves four more people. One, Ms. Washington Bay, two, President Mitchell—but we'll save him for our grand finale. Let me see. Three, I'm thinking one of the professors. A professor that everyone hates but is well known."

Jeremy rubbing his hands. "Actually, I don't think that will matter. If you kill any professor, it will scare the all the other professors on campus into thinking that they better be careful how they treat the students in their classes. All the students will know that the killings have caused this change in the professors' behavior. So I think we should choose a random professor and the last person that we need to kill before President Mitchell is Matthew Juice, the president of the Alpha Alpha Alpha Fraternity."

Richard nodded. "Wow! I didn't even think about the impact of the fraternities on campus. You got this thing down to a science. Every male on campus at one time wanted to be in Alpha Alpha Alpha. Or at least I know I did, but they are so picky in their candidates. But then again, they are one of the most popular frats on campus, so I guess they can be picky."

I slapped Richard and Jeremy on the legs. "It's settled. We'll go to the Homecoming game tonight to see who is crowned Ms. Washington Bay and we'll make plans to kill her when we get back here. Only four more people to get rid of and then we're on to a better life."

#

Six

I turned on the news as I was going through my closet to pick out something to wear. My mouth dropped as one of the reporters said that the police had found a bag with three bloody gowns in it near the Paddy Foot dorm. The police were going through every single room in Paddy Foot to see if they could tie anyone to the bag. Good thing we didn't leave that bag near our dorm. I turned the channel to another news station and there was a little information on how some of Washington Bay's Homecoming events were cancelled because of the murders. The story was interrupted by breaking news. A black lady with silky long hair announced with her eyes wide, that the police had found a broken machete in the Sandal Foot dorm room.

Oh yes, I had forgotten all about that machete. Melvin's late entrance had messed up my train of thought after killing the black girl with braids. If Melvin had never shown up, or better yet, come before the girl, Richard, Jeremy and I would have never left any evidence. I shook my head and turned to yet another news channel. The story about Melvin scrolled across the bottom of the screen as the news reporters spoke about a missing girl named Jessica. Her picture came onscreen, revealing a smiling blonde girl in her late teens. The police believed Jessica was murdered and the killer had dumped her body somewhere. Jessica was a sophomore attending summer school on Washington Bay campus before her disappearance about three months prior to Mrs. Sternverger's and Melvin's murders. The police believed Jessica was dead because they received a call about a possible homicide at the Alpha Alpha Alpha frat house. When the police arrived, all they found was blood all over the bathroom, along with some cow manure and gravel. I was surprised that the police never found Jessica's body or the person that called 911, not to mention relieved. Maybe, forensics science wasn't as tough to beat as I thought. The reporter said the police were trying to see if there were any links between the possible murder of Jessica Simmons and the Washington Bay Vampire killings.

Once I was dressed for the game, I headed over to Jeremy's room to go to the game together. Outside our dorm, we saw at four police cars parked in front of our dorm and two officers on the front walkway. They were stopping people as they walked by to ask them question. All the guys loitering around the dorms and even the guys walking by were wearing Melvin's Jersey. Even some of the girls were wearing Jersey dresses with Melvin's numbers on them. Some of the cars that in the parking lot had Melvin's numbers spray painted on the side windows above messages like "*We'll miss you, big Mel*" and "*The Long Arm Ranger lives on.*"

We walked past the cops on our way to the stadium across campus. One of the cops, a short and skinny white man, stopped us. "Heading to the game, huh? It'll never be the same without Long Arm Melvin."

I forced myself to sigh and say, "Yeah. I know. The guy was a legend."

The cop nodded. "You boys see anything strange or any strange people lurking around your dorm last night? Anyone that you find a little strange?"

Jeremy smirked. "Everyone is strange in their own way."

Richard tapped Jeremy on the shoulder, chuckling. "No, just you, Jeremy."

The cop stared at Richard and Jeremy with a serious expression the whole time they spoke to him. Then he handed each of us a card and said, "Well, if you boys know about or hear about any information that may lead us to whoever did this crime, please, don't hesitate to give me a call."

Richard, Jeremy, and I continued towards the stadium. We crossed a field filled with a waiting crowd. Homecoming on Washington Bay campus was a money market and nearly everyone from the surrounding neighborhoods was selling. Vendors were set up along the sidewalks around nearly half the campus, not to mention in designated areas set up for booths.

People browsed the vendors' offerings. There were students passing out fliers for parties and other homecoming. Along the sidewalks that lead to the entrance of the stadium, there were lots of people selling foods, DVD's, cd's, Washington Bay t-shirts, and other items. It was only 6:30pm and the stadium was almost full, even though, the game didn't start till 7pm. The parking lot section designated for trailers was full, with people parking on the grass between the sidewalk and parking lot. Richard, Jeremy, and I walked through the vendors and got in one of three long lines that lead into the stadium. I glanced at some of the events posted on the flyer I received. "So what do you guys want to do after the game? Want to hit up one of these clubs?"

Jeremy shook his head. "I don't think so. I'll just probably go home after all of this is over. I hate going to clubs."

I rubbed the back of my neck. "I just figured since it was Homecoming, maybe we should do something different. Like normal college students for a change. Everyone is going out tonight. There will be a lot of drunken women at the clubs. Maybe they'll be drunk enough to give us some booty tonight."

Richard said, "Well, why not? After we find out who Ms. Washington Bay is and the game ends, we don't have much else to do tonight. Wasup, Jeremy?"

Jeremy grunted. "Naw. I'm alright. You guys have fun. I'm going to pass on this one. I think it's just a waste of time."

A tall, blond guy standing in the middle line next to us tapped me on the shoulder. "I don't mean to eavesdrop, but why do you guys want to know who Ms. Washington Bay is?"

Jeremy squinted, hostilely. "Why do you care?"

I said, "Well, one of my friends is a candidate for Ms. Washington Bay. I hope she wins."

The blond guy said, "Who is she?"

I smirked. "Well, you know, the dirty blonde girl. I can't believe I can't remember her name right now. We were just talking about her. Don't you just hate that when your brain freezes up like that, and you can't remember the name of someone that you speak with all the time?"

The blond haired guy said, "There is no dirty blonde candidate. All three are brunettes."

I scratched my head, "Well. You know, sometimes when girls have brown hair it may look blonde depending on how light or dark the brown is. I thought she was blonde. I guess she has brown hair, then."

The guy said, "I guess," and turned back to his two friends who were in deep conversation next to him in line.

We made it into the stadium, got our seats and watched the first half of the game. Washington Bay was killing Howard with Washington bay scoring 21 points to Howard only scoring 6 points in the first half. Some people left the stands to go home, other went to get refreshments, and some frat members were passing out flyers to people in the stands. Richard, Jeremy, and I stayed glued in our seat to wait for the crowning of Ms. Washington Bay during the half time show.

After the Cheer leaders danced and the band played a few selections, the booth announcer announced who got the most votes for Mr. Washington Bay. Our student council president, Derrick Meters, who I had only heard of but never met, was crowned.

Next they announced the candidates and crowned Rachel Williams as Ms. Washington Bay. Rachel Williams was a gorgeous Hispanic woman on Washington Bay's swim team. I had seen her a few times here and there around campus. The only reason that I knew she was on the swim team was because the school newspaper had her on the front page of their paper when she broke a state record in the women's 100 meter freestyle. I wrote her name down on a piece of paper from my pocket. "Dang. She's hot, man."

She was five foot five with brown hair, a thin waist, balloon breasts, and a plump butt. She had green eyes and lips like Angelina Jolie.

Richard smiled. "I know, man. I wonder who her lucky boyfriend is. Goodness."

A familiar voice behind us said, "You boys keep eyeing my girl like that and you won't be able to go to Alpha Alpha Alpha's party tonight."

I turned around and grinned at the blond guy that had talked to us earlier in line. "You're a lucky man. I wish I had a girl like that."

He nodded. "You have no idea at all. By the way, my name is Larry Prickings. I'm the new Alpha Alpha Alpha president."

 "What happened to Matthew Mitchell?"

Larry said, "He transferred to Michigan State. Anyway, we have a dope party going on at our fraternity house tonight. It's forty dollars a person. Free drinks. Lots of women. You won't find any party anywhere else like the one at our house tonight, so don't miss out Here, take some flyers. Give some to your friends. I'll see you boys there."

Larry gave me and Richard some dap and extended his hand to Jeremy, who crossed his arms. "Well, go fuck yourself then."

Jeremy glared at Larry and reached in his side pocket as if he was clutching something. "What you want to do?"

Larry's frat brothers jumped between Jeremy and Larry and pulled Larry away from us. I grabbed Jeremy's arm. "Relax. He was just saying wasup."

Jeremy grunted, "I'd like to cut his intestines out."

Richard said, "Well, you just might get the chance."

People sitting in front of us were turning around to look with screwed-up faces displaying their disgust with Jeremy's talk. Richard and I got up to escort Jeremy out of the stadium as he shouted, "What ya'll looking at? Mind your own business. I'll cut ya'll too!"

It was around 9pm and nearly all the vendors had gone home. The sidewalks and streets were nearly empty. There was trash and flyers scattered all over the sidewalks and streets. I waited till we were alone a little distance away from the stadium a and then I sternly said to Jeremy, "you are really losing it. You're threatening people in the midst of crowded places. Are you crazy? Right after all this coverage on the news?"

Richard said, "Yeah. Everyone has seen your face. If the cops ask any of those people if they've seen anyone strange, they are going to point in your direction."

Jeremy smirked. "None of those people know my name. They barely pay me any attention on campus. I could have been going to this school for three years and been in every class with everyone one of those people and none of them would remember me. I might as well be invisible to people as snobbish as them. They won't remember what I look like. They're too much into themselves to pay my plain face enough attention to remember the small details."

I shook my head. "Let's not get arrogant. Remember, we're not done yet. We still have four more…you know what to pull off."

Richard nodded. "Yeah. Now that police probably have our DNA from those gowns they, we have to be extra careful no one is able to identify us as the killers."

I put my finger over my lips. "Let's save the talking till we get back to Jeremy's room. Anybody could be out here listening."

When we got back to Jeremy's room, we discussed possibly following Rachel home from the Alpha Alpha Alpha party.

Richard and I were able to convince Jeremy that the Alpha Alpha Alpha party would provide the perfect opportunity to kill Rachel, or at least to find out some information about where she was staying.

After playing some Madden and watching television for a while, Jeremy, Richard and I left Jeremy's room a little after 11pm to head to the Alpha Alpha Alpha House near campus.

When we arrived, there were people standing outside of the frat house drinking beer and sitting in lawn chairs. There were empty plastic cups scattered all over the front yard of the triple Alpha house. There was a triple Alpha cooking barbecue in the driveway. There was music playing in the house so loud it could be heard outside. There had to be about fifty people or more in front of the house, on the lawn and near the curb.

The triple Alpha house was a humongous red brick house with three floors. On the front porch, four tall columns held up part of the third story bedrooms. On the first floor, the curtains were open and the blinds were pulled up so that you could see people dancing and sitting on the couches. Jeremy, Richard, and I walked through the field of people and squeezed through the front door among a constant stream of people going in and out of it. The first floor lights were dim, except in the kitchen. Richard, Jeremy and I walked through the crowded living room, where people were dancing to music, to head into the kitchen. There was a keg on the kitchen table and empty beer cans all over the kitchen counters. There were about ten to fifteen people seated or standing around a beer keg on the kitchen table. Some of the people were cheering as others were drinking down large mugs filled with beer. As we approached the table, a familiar voice said, "Make yourselves at home. We have more beer in the fridge or you can pour some out of the keg."

We all looked over at Larry as he walked toward us. I extended my hand and Larry shook it. Larry shook hands with Richard as well and extended his hand to Jeremy. "No grudges. Let's start over. Let me get you a drink."

Jeremy shook Larry's hand and we all sat at the table. Larry poured cups for Richard, Jeremy and I. I was a bit shy around everyone, as I hadn't really been to a party in a long time. But everyone greeted Jeremy, Richard and I and started some small talk with each of us. We started to talk about our classes, our plans after college, comedians, celebrities and lots of random topics. We all began to drink and the beer had loosened up Jeremy, Richard and I until we felt like we were around childhood friends.

As the hours passed, most of the people at the table got up and left to who knows where. Finally, Richard, Jeremy, myself, and Larry with two of his friends were the only ones left at the table. The disc jockey had stopped for the night and there were very few people out in the dining room making even a small amount of noise. Richard was passed out asleep in his chair. Jeremy sat across from me and rested his chair against the wall, wide awake. As Larry was chatting to me about celebrity crushes and how he would like to fondle Britney Spears' breasts. One of Larry's friends, a short, red-haired guy, gave Larry some dap and extended his hand to me. "The name is Jake, if you forgot…you're Greg…right? Your friend that's sleeping is Richard… Nice to meet you, again."

Jake nodded to Jeremy as he moved on. "Nice to meet you, too, Jeremy."

Larry's other friend, a light skinned Hispanic guy with a ponytail, got up and nodded at Jeremy, Richard and me. "The name is Eric. Nice to meet you guys."

Larry and I changed the subject, trying to decide the top five rappers of all time. As I was telling Larry about Eminem's new album, Rachel walked in the kitchen and sat next to Larry. Larry introduced Jeremy and me to Rachel. The dress was so tight I could see Rachel's nipples pressing through the jersey. I congratulated her on her win as Ms. Washington Bay and she smiled. "Thank you."

She grabbed Larry's hand and said, "I didn't mean to disturb you guys, I just wanted to tell you that I'm going out to a club in Miami with a few of my friends. The Sorority Delta Delta Delta rented a party bus for the weekend to hit a few clubs in Miami. My friends and I are going to head over to the Triple Delta sorority house to ride the bus. I'll be back at the apartment in a couple of hours."

Larry gave Rachel a peck on the lips that turned into French kissing for at least ten seconds. Rachel and Larry looked at me, smiling. I smirked. "Get a room, please."

Rachel wiped her mouth. "Sorry. I'm slobbing everywhere."

She extended her left hand and I sighed as I looked at her hand with spit in it. She chuckled, wiped her hand on Larry's shirt and then shook with her right hand. "Nice to meet you, Tom."

"It's Greg."

Rachel rolled her eyes and began walking off. "Yeah. Whatever it is."

Jeremy smirked. "Bye, Rachel."

Rachel turned to look at Jeremy with a frown, hissing, "See ya. Never."

Jeremy shook his head, stood up and tapped me on the shoulder. "I'm going to go to the bathroom, I'll be right back."

Larry closed his eyes, smiling. I told him, "I think you had too much beer. Let me take that glass from you."

Larry looked up at me. "I love that girl. I have had girls that were just as fine as Rachel, but I never have had a girl that was as polite. You see how she came by just to tell me that she was going out with her friends, so I wouldn't suspect she was out with another guy. She might make the perfect wife."

I grinned. "I see what you mean. But how does he treat Eric and Jake? Your other friends, while we're at it?"

Larry shrugged. "She always seems pretty polite to my friends.

Larry leaned across the table. "I just hope she'll be okay, going out late. You know, with those crazy people on the loose. Killing people in dorm rooms. I think they are called the Vampires. I just hope the Vampires don't hurt Rachel."

I nodded. "It's not just the vampires that you need to be worried about. They only kill people at their homes. I was watching the news earlier and they were talking about a girl named Jessica that went missing on campus about three months ago. And this was at a party. Actually at a triple Alpha party, if I remember correctly. Rachel's actually safer being away from this frat house than at a club."

Larry began to study his nails. "I guess. Everyone thinks that my frat brothers had something to do with Jessica's murder. The whole thing is ruining our name. The stupid girl was a slut anyway. She shouldn't have been such a tease, coming on to my frat brothers all the time. That stupid broad had the nerve to tell me no. No one tells me no. I'm happy she's dead."

Larry shook his head. "Her body is probably rotting under some gravel next to this house. I hope the worms eat her flesh. Should a stabbed her one more time."

My eyes widen and my right arm is shaking. I hold my breath as Larry grabs the plastic cup from my hand, refills the cup from the keg and gulps down its contents. "I got to go the bathroom, I'll be right back."

I release my breath as Larry leaves the room. What a creep! I look over at Richard, who is still passed out on the table. Jeremy comes back with his arm wrapped around a drunken brunette. They sit at the table and Jeremy says, "This is Sarah. Sarah, this is Greg."

Sarah is a short, skinny girl with big boobs and brown eyes. She leans over the table and slurs, "You are so handsome, Gregory. Do you have some vitamin D for me?"

Sarah pulled herself onto the table and tried to kiss me. Jeremy smiled and pulled Sarah back into her seat by grabbing the belt on her tight jeans. Sarah chuckled and mumbled to Jeremy, "I'm so glad that I have a nice, strong man to keep me from drinking too much. You know you shouldn't drink too much. It's bad for you."

Sarah kissed Jeremy and turned to throw up on the table. Some of the vomit landed on Richard's face and woke him up. He brushed the throw up off his face. "Smells like spoiled milk and hot dogs."

Sarah grabbed Jeremy's shirt and wiped her mouth. "Sorry, honey. I'll make it up to you."

Richard left the room, I think to go to the bathroom.

Sarah whispered to Jeremy, "Let's get a room upstairs."

Larry returned to the kitchen. "Jesus Christ. Not all over my table!"

Sarah came over to Larry and gave him a hug, "I'm so, so, sorry. Let me clean it up for you, babe."

Sarah unbuttoned her blouse and took it off. She kissed Larry on the cheek and then starts to wipe the table with her blouse.

Jeremy grabbed Sarah's arm. "Let me get that for you. Why don't you sit back down until I get done and then we'll go upstairs?"

Larry grunted. "Oh no, no one is doing anything in any of the rooms upstairs."

Sarah gagged and threw up again, this time on a chair next to the table.

Larry shouted, "Sarah, look what you're doing! Out of my house!"

Sarah went to Larry and tried to wipe her mouth off with his shirt.

Larry screamed, "Get your nasty mouth away from me!"

Sarah fell on her knees and wiped her mouth against Larry's pants leg.

Larry moved his leg away and Sarah began to unbutton her pants. "Let me clean that up for you."

Jeremy walked over, picked Sarah up by the waist and grinned at Larry. "Let's go upstairs. All three of us."

I smirked at Larry. "I'll clean up the mess. Go have fun."

Jeremy, Larry, and Sarah left to go upstairs. I got a wash cloth from the sink in the kitchen and began to clean up the throw up. It took me an hour or so to clean up the vomit and I didn't see Richard, Larry, Jeremy or Sarah the whole time. I scoped out the first floor and found out that nearly everyone, including the triple Alpha brothers, had left to go home. The only people left in the house were Richard, Jeremy, Larry, Sarah and I. Richard was sleeping on the couch in the living room. I sat beside him and turned on the television. Larry walked down stairs into the living room, wearing nothing but his pants and socks. "You still here? Sarah is still in the bed with Jeremy, sleeping. If you want a piece of her, you should go up there and get you some before all the alcohol that she had wears off."

I shook my head. "I'll pass this time."

Larry sat down into a love seat next to the couch. "Don't tell Rachel about this. She'll kill me, if she ever finds out. You're not a snitch, are you?"

I shook my head.

"Good. Don't tell anyone. Especially anything that I told you dealing with Jessica. I don't want to have to…just don't talk to anyone about it."

I nodded. "I got it."

I nearly jumped out of my seat when I heard screaming coming from upstairs. Larry and I ran upstairs to the bathroom door, where all the noise was coming from. Sarah was shouting, "Get off of me. Don't touch me."

Larry checked the door and found it was locked. He started throwing his shoulder into the door until it gave way. Jeremy was lying on top of Sarah, butt naked. There were bleeding scratch marks all over his back. Sarah had on a bra, but her panties had been pulled down to her ankles. She was scratching Jeremy across his back as she wiggled violently, crying and screaming, "Get off me! Pleaaaassseee! Stop! Stop! Pleaaasssse!" Jeremy grabbed her throat with his left hand as he thrust in her and moaned, "You dumb bitch! Shut the fuck up, you stupid ho!"

Sarah's sobbing and tears intensified with each of Jeremy's strokes. Jeremy turned to face us as I shouted, "Jeremy what are you doing? Get off of her!" Sarah squirmed from under Jeremy as he turned to face Larry and me. She stood up and ran past us out the bathroom door. Jeremy yelled, "Get her, Greg. She's going to ruin everything!"

I ran down the stairs after Sarah and pushed her hard against the front door as she tried to unlock it. Sarah fell to the floor and I got on top of her to pin her. I covered her mouth and put her in a rear naked choke as Jeremy came down the stairs with Larry trailing behind him. Sarah wiggled savagely Jeremy began pulling down the blinds and closing all the curtains on the first floor.

Larry walked over to the couch, picked up his cell phone and said, "I don't want to take any part in this. I'm calling the police."

As Larry was unlocking his phone, I screamed, "I'm going to tell them about Jessica if you call the cops. I'm going to tell the where she's buried under the gravel near a farm not that far from here."

Larry's face turned red and he hung up the phone. Jeremy went into the kitchen and came back out with a butcher knife. "Look out, Greg!"

I let Sarah go and she wiggled from under me. As she tried to get up, Jeremy kneeled down and stabbed Sarah through the back. She fell to the floor and Jeremy viciously stabbed Sarah.

Larry sat down into a corner and rolled over into fetal position, crying, "Oh, dear Lord. What did you do? ...I can't."

Jeremy wiped the blade across his shirt and tossed it to me. "Finish him."

I murmured, "What now?....Richard is asleep, man...Rachel, Eric and tons of people know….saw us here with Larry. They'll identify us."

Jeremy shook his head. "Then hand me the knife, son."

I tossed Jeremy the knife and he began walking towards Larry. I grabbed Jeremy around the waist. "Jeremy. Another time. He's not going to say anything. I got dirt on him. No one saw us with Sarah. As far as everyone else knows, some stranger at the party killed her in the bathroom upstairs."

Jeremy dropped the knife, walked over to Larry and kneeled beside him. "You didn't see anything. You were sleeping on the couch and when you woke up, you had to use the bathroom and that's when you found Sarah, dead in your bathroom. The first thing you did was call 911. There were so many people at your party that it could have been anyone. Now, you stay here while Greg and I clean up this mess. I don't want your DNA on her."

Jeremy and I picked up Sarah and carried her to the bathroom. I pressed down on her chest to make a pool of blood around her body. I took off my shoes and washed the blood from them in the sink. Jeremy went into Larry's room and put on his clothes. I grabbed a towel from the bathroom closet and wiped away the bloody foot- and shoeprints in the bathroom and hall. I rinsed the towel in the sink and walked downstairs with Jeremy to wipe the streaks of blood off the front door and walls. Larry had fainted on the floor near the couch. I rung the bloody towel out in the kitchen and grabbed a mop to clean up the pool of blood near the door. Jeremy woke up Richard and unlocked the front door. Jeremy, Richard and I left the frat house and began to jog home, leaving Larry still asleep on the floor. Jeremy threw the butcher knife down a sewer drain nearby. I unbuttoned my shirt that had blood all over it. I balled the bloody shirt up into a ball and carried it in my right hand.

When we reached our dorm, Jeremy whispered, "At my place, first thing in morning."

#

Seven

I tossed and turned most of the night. Every noise that I heard sounded like the police standing outside, ready to kick my door in and arrest me for Sarah's murder. I fell asleep after a few hours,

I woke up and turned on my television. The news was covering Sarah's murder at the triple Alpha frat house. The news reporters were trying to connect Sarah's murder to Jessica's murder. Another reporter interrupted the coverage with breaking news that the police had Larry Prickings as a suspect in custody. Police believed that Larry brutally stabbed Sarah to death in the bathroom, but they needed more investigation to confirm their allegations. I took a shower before heading over to Jeremy's room. Richard was already watching the news with Jeremy.

I shut the door behind me. "I guess you guys heard by now, huh? I just want to know, Jeremy. What happened? You were upstairs for at least an hour, Larry comes down bragging about how you guys ran a train on the girl and then all of a sudden, I hear Sarah screaming for dear life from the bathroom."

Jeremy turned his chair around to face me. "Everything was fine at first. Larry and I took turns having sex with Sarah. I went into his bedroom first and nailed her and then I came out and Larry went in. Larry had been in the room with her for almost thirty minute and I was getting worried so I walked in. Larry was passed out asleep next to Sarah, under the covers. I took off my clothes again and slid in the bed next to her and fell asleep for about ten minutes. I woke up because I felt too hot, lying next to Sarah. When I woke up, Larry had left the room and I started to think about how good the sex was earlier that night. So I started to kiss on Sarah's neck and she woke up. Sarah jumped up and looked around the room like she didn't know where she was at. Sarah looked at me and said, 'I have to go to the bathroom really quick.' I sat in bed a couple of minutes waiting for her and then I walked to the bathroom. I put my ear to the door and heard snoring, so I walked in, and I saw Sarah was passed out, sitting on the toilet seat with her pants down. I locked the door, kneeled on the floor near Sarah and kissed her on the cheek. I picked up Sarah and laid her on the floor. I began to have sex with Sarah and she woke up. Sarah began to push me off of her and scream, 'Get off me, no!' I tried to stop myself, Greg, but I was almost at the point of orgasm. I couldn't resist it. It was too good, so I held her arms down and continued having sex with her as she wrestled with me. I didn't mean for it to happen. I feel bad about it, man. I'm just glad that you had my back. I'm sorry, man. I know I let you guys down and maybe even ruined this whole operation that we had going. Don't worry, Greg. I'll take the whole charge myself. You and Richard had nothing to do with it. You both were downstairs asleep and if Forensics catches us altering the murder scene, I'll say that I moved the body to the bathroom and that I threatened to kill you guys if you called the cops. You and Richard feared for your lives."

I put my hand on Jeremy's shoulder. "I forgive you, man. Maybe Larry won't talk. He knows that I have dirt on him. Maybe that will keep him from snitching on us. At least I hope so."

Richard said, "Well no matter what, I think what is most important is that whoever is still free after Sarah's murder boils over should continue with our plans. Otherwise we did all those murders in vain. At least someone can reap the benefits of our hard work."

I nodded. "Maybe we should wait a week or so before we continue our plans. For all we know, the police, the F.B.I., could be monitoring our every move."

Jeremy shook his head. "We have to continue. There is not much time. The news has been covering these murders almost every day. The people in the community want closure to all this. With that much pressure on the police, they're using every resource possible to solve these murders. All it takes is one good lead or a piece of evidence that we left behind, and we're caught. If I have to, I'll sit out the next murder or two. But we need follow through with our plans."

We continued to watch the news story on Sarah's murder for an hour or so until it went off in favor of a story about a robbery that took place at a gas station in Miami. I challenged Jeremy to play me in some Madden. A few minutes into playing Madden, Jeremy paused the Game., "I just thought of something…..the police are working hard on solving these murders and may be closing in on us, and our body count isn't that high. If you remember from the DVD, Jeffrey Dahmer stood out among the other serial killers because a large number of bodies were found stashed in his house."

I shook my head, "So you're thinking that we should plan a mass killing? Didn't you just say that you'll sit out the next murder or two? Now you're talking about planning a mass murder."

Jeremy nodded. "I did talk about taking a small break, but now, rethinking things, our time may be limited. We just need to lure a bunch of people to a place that is hidden, where no one can hear them scream and we need to find a way to kill them without them ganging up on us."

"Yeah, it's going to be very easy to find and lure a bunch of people who are gullible enough to walk into an isolated area, unarmed and defenseless," I said, rolling my eyes.

Richard said, "How about we sneak into the shower room in the female dormitory on the top floor, and kill a bunch of women as they shower in the morning, before going to class?"

Jeremy and I looked at each other and then at Richard. "Naw," Jeremy said.

I said, "There is too much security at the dorms as a result of the Melvin's murder." Jeremy tapped me on the arm. "I got it! You remember what Rachel said to Larry last night before she left? She said that the triple Delta sorority rented a party bus for the weekend. They are using the bus to escort people to the parties in Miami. The length of the expressway strip between here and Miami just might provide an opportunity for us to isolate the people on the bus and murder them without any interference from the police. If the bus pulls off the side of the road, People driving by might just think that the bus has a flat tire. Plus, if we can carry this out tonight, there won't be a lot of people on the road. Most people should be at home preparing for work in the morning. The trick will be how to get the bus to pull over to the side of the road and how to keep the girls from calling the police on their cell phones. Maybe we can find a way to drug them before they leave for the party."

I leaned back in my chair, "I've got an even better way. I saw this in a movie once. If you stuff up the exhaust pipe on the bus, the carbon monoxide will seep into the vehicle through the vents. Carbon monoxide is odorless and very undetectable. In twenty minutes or so, everyone will pass out from breathing in the fumes. It takes an hour to get to downtown Miami. The bus will crash over to the side of the road before then. We just need to hope that the bus driver doesn't pass out with his foot on the accelerator. Hopefully, after he's out the bus will drift over to either side of the road, without flipping over, hitting a few cars or falling off into a ditch."

Jeremy sat back in his chair. "That sounds great, but how will we be able to enter a bus filled with carbon monoxide?"

"We could steal some smoke masks from the Chemistry lab in Tucker hall" Richard said. "They usually leave the doors open at Tucker Hall, but I'm sure that the Chemistry lab rooms are locked. My professor always locks the door, when my classmates and I leave lab. We can pick the lock, though, and steal the masks."

Jeremy stood up. "Sounds like a plan. We'll leave around 8pm to steal the mask and then we'll head over to the sorority house and wait until the party bus shows up. Then we'll plug up the exhaust and follow the bus as it heads to Miami."

Richard and I looked at each other and smiled and then nodded at Jeremy. Jeremy resumed the game. We continued playing Madden for a few hours, before Richard and I headed back to our own dorm rooms.

At a quarter to 8pm, I met back up with Jeremy in his dorm room. Richard had been hanging out with Jeremy for the past half hour and they were in the middle of playing Madden, when I arrived. I stood at the door, as Richard turned off the game and Jeremy filled his book bag with a hammer, the fangers, a lock pick set, our costumes, and some knives.

Jeremy pulled out a container of clay out his drawer, "I bought this earlier at Target; we can stuff this in the exhaust pipe. We'll need someone to distract the driver before he pulls up at the sorority house."

Richard raised his hand. "I'll do it."

"Great! And I'll stuff the exhaust pipe, while you wait in the car for us, Greg. We'll park at a distance from the house, so that we aren't seen." Jeremy put the container of clay in his book bag.

We headed out the door and walked across campus to Tucker hall. We walked around the building to look for any bystanders and waited on a bench, nearby, until the coast was clear. We opened an unlocked side door and snuck into the building. We headed to the second floor and

stopped at the lab, where Richard has class. I wiggled the door and found it locked. Jeremy took

out the lock pick set and tried to unlock the door, to no avail. There was a deadbolt lock above

the door knob that the pick couldn't quite unlock.

Richard said, "Step back!"

He began kicking the door, and after a few minutes it gave in. the door swung open, with

wood debris scattering across the room.

Jeremy ran into the room. "Let's hurry before the Janitor or someone catches us!"

We sprinted to a metallic cabinet in the back that had a lock on it.

Richard pointed at the cabinet. "The masks are in there."

Jeremy took out the hammer from his bag and beat on the lock until it broke apart.

I opened the cabinet doors and we each grabbed a smoke mask. We ran out of the lab and

downstairs, out the door. We walked to my car, in front of the dorm. We put the masks in the

trunk and drove to the sorority house. We parked a block away from the on the same side of the

street. 9:30pm blinked on my clock display as we sat watching the group of girls standing by a

car that sat in front of the triple Delta house. Ten minutes later, I heard a rumbling noise coming

from a distance behind us. I turned around and saw a bus heading our way.

Jeremy said, "That's probably the bus. Richard, you get out and wave down the bus for

directions. I'm going to walk down the sidewalk and as you talk to the bus driver, I'm going to

put the clay in the exhaust of the tail pipe."

Jeremy grabbed his book bag and got out the car. Richard also got out and began walking

down the middle of the street, waving at the bus driver. The bus slowed down and Richard talked

with the bus driver, as Jeremy snuck up. After a few minutes, Jeremy walked from behind the bus, back onto the sidewalk. The bus pulled off ahead as Richard stepped back, saluting the driver. Jeremy strutted towards the car. The bus parked in front of the Triple Delta house, behind the group of girls in front of the house and honked the horn. Richard and Jeremy ran towards my car and hopped in.

Jeremy grinned. "I did it! Let's hope that the girl's get in and get on the road before the bus driver passes out."

A few minutes later, a large group of girls came out of the house and boarded the bus. The bus was all black with tinted windows and a large pink company logo across the side that read: *The Thomas Sterling Party Bus: A VIP Experience.*

The bus took off and we followed it onto the expressway. There was barely any traffic on the road, at that time. We saw a few cars, every two miles or so. The expressway had a concrete median and lots of grass fields, woods, and concrete walls on either side. Twenty minutes went by and the bus swerved from the left lane to the right as its speed decreased. The bus brushed against the concrete median for about ten seconds, causing the two left tires to flatten. The bus came to a halt. We pulled over to the side of the road thirty feet in front of the bus. Jeremy pulled out our costumes from the bag and we put them on. A few cars with bright headlights passed our car as Jeremy handed us each a knife and a fanger.

Jeremy said, "Let's make this quick and head out before any police or tow-trucks show up."

We looked down the road to see if any cars were coming, and when the road was clear for several miles, we jumped out and opened the trunk. We ripped open the veils covering our faces and put on the smoke masks before sprinting to the bus. Richard kicked in the sliding door and pulled it open. The bus driver was passed out against the steering wheel and there was loud music playing. We walked up the stairs and saw several girls passed out on the leather couch seats, between the seats, and on top of one another. Most of the 16 girls on the bus were passed out, while others were in the middle of seizures or drunkenly laying on the floor, barely moving and talking to themselves. There was a stripper pole in the middle of the bus and several strobe lights sitting in the corners. There were lots of flicking lights on the ceiling and speakers planted in the walls. A house music song was playing and the singer on the track sung, "*We're going to have a good time* tonight, *oh yeah, a good time tonight.*" Jeremy went to the back of the bus and starting dancing as he stabbed a seizing girl in the stomach. Richard stabbed the bus driver in the neck and I felt the warm droplets of blood splattered onto my gown. I turned off the engine and the music stopped playing. Richard and I walked into the middle of the bus and began cutting open the stomachs of the girls at random. Blood flew everywhere. There was blood on the windows, on the ceiling, all over our gowns and smoke masks, on the leather couches and carpet. I slashed one of the girls passed out on the couch, across her DD boobs and silicone oozed down her shirt mixed in blood. I turned towards the stripper pole and saw a red hair girl wiggling around slowly the ground with her face to the ground. I stabbed her in the back of the neck and my knife got stuck. I put my foot on her back and yanked out the knife, causing her spine to protrude from her neck. We heard screaming from the back and saw Jeremy wrestling with a girl that became partly conscious. Jeremy slapped the girl and she fell to the ground. Richard and I walked toward Jeremy to help, but Jeremy yelled, "I got her."

I pulled a girl off another girl to see if I had killed that one already and I did. I then knelt down to the floor and check through the pile of girls for any that were still alive. Richard followed suit, searching through the pile of women on the leather couch across of me. We heard a grunting sound coming from the back of the bus and heard the screaming of a girl. I peered into the back and saw Jeremy on top of the girl that he had been wrestling with. The girl was on the

floor, on her stomach with no pants and Jeremy had his pants pulled down. Jeremy thrusted in

the girl as she tried to wiggle from under him and he pulled her hair, violently. The girl pushed

off Jeremy and kicked him in the nuts. Richard shook his head and ripped the intestines out of

the dead girls in front of him to toss them across the room. I took a step towards Jeremy, but then

stopped and took a stepped back. The girl got up and Jeremy grabbed her leg, causing her to

crash into the side of the bus. The girl braced herself from falling by placing her hands against

the wall and Jeremy used his grip on her leg to pull himself up. Jeremy smashed the girl's head

against the wall. He grabbed her with one arm and used his other hand to insert his jimmy into

the girl from behind, as he used his shoulder and body weight to pin her to the wall. After

pumping into the girl several times, Jeremy put the girl in a rear naked choke and choked her

until she passed out. Jeremy continued to pump the girl until he came inside her. I just stood

there, shaking my head as Jeremy finished feeding his steamy appetite. Jeremy slammed the girl

to the ground, pulled up his pants and looked at me, "What? Let's finish before the cops come!" I

Snatched out the intestines of a brunette girl and wrote our usual message on the tinted windows

in blood. Jeremy shouted, "Let's go, it's been at least fifteen minutes. I'm surprised that no cops

or any tow people have shown up yet." We looked through the back window to see if any cars

were headed towards us and when the coast was clear, when ran off the bus and dove into my

car. We drove up a few exits and got off to turn around and head back down the expressway in

the opposite direction. We took each of our masks and Jeremy and Richard took off their gowns

to put them in the book bag. On the way home, we looked across the median and saw several

police cars and a tow truck parked around the party bus. The lane near the bus was blocked off

with cones and there were road flares planted nearby. The traffic across from us had slowed down and several police officers stood around the bus. We got out of there in the nick of time. As

we headed home, we stopped in an alley, behind a closed Food Lion Supermarket. I took off my

gown and put it in the book bag, along with the knives that we used on the bus. We dumped the

masks and the book bag in the Food Lion garbage bin. I opened the top and jumped into the bin.

I covered the book bag and masks with several filled trashed bags and collapsed boxes. We

hopped back into the car and drove to our dorm. Jeremy said, "I can't believe that we pulled that

off. That was awesome."

Richard and I said, at the same time, "I know."

Jeremy sighed, "Let's get some sleep! We'll discuss everything about tonight, tomorrow,

after classes, in my room."

We walked up to our rooms to crash for the night. We now had an additional sixteen

deaths added to our body count. What a way to end the homecoming weekend. We represented.

We would sleep well tonight. Sweet Dreams!

The next day, after class, I went to Jeremy's room and found both Jeremy and Richard

watching the news. The newscaster shook her head. "The Washington Bay Vampires strike again.

Last night, the police found a party bus crashed along the median on the I95 expressway. The

police stepped onto the bus to find several Triple Delta sorority women slaughtered on the bus.

The police believe that the women were victims of the Washington Bay Vampires, the same

serial killers that killed the beloved football player, Melvin Peters. The police stated that they do

not having any suspects at the moment, but know that the Washington Bay Vampires were

responsible from the graphic message that they left on the bus in blood. Sixteen women were

murdered on the bus and police said that the bus was filled with carbon monoxide. Someone had

filled the exhaust pipe with clay. Carbon Monoxide seeped into the bus, which caused the death of half of the women and caused several others to pass out before they were killed. The police are unsure if the Vampires put the clay in the exhaust pipe, but we will be sure to update you on this event as the investigation continues and we receive more information."

Jeremy turned off the television and gave Richard a high five. "We're on our way, man!"

Jeremy gave me a high five and hugged me. "If we keep this up, we might go down as the most grisly serial killers of all time. Now that we have more than enough kills to be considered serial killers, and we have set ourselves apart from most serial killers with this mass killing, we just completed, we need to build our legacy. We can possibly be scarier than Charles Mason and more gruesome than Jeffrey Dahmer, if we finish our plans to kill off the infamous people that we discussed. The mass killing will cause nationwide coverage, but to stay relevant nationwide and possibly hit news in London and France, we need to draw the nation's interest into learning about us and into finding out who we are and why we do the things we do. The deaths of Melvin Peters and Mrs. Sternverger made great headlines and brought us lots of infamy, but we will need more infamy to surpass the great serial killers like Ted Bundy."

I nodded, "I agree, but we need to be careful about this. We almost got caught yesterday, mainly because we didn't plan carefully enough to know how often the police patrol the expressway and where they usually are posted."

Richard tapped me on the arm. "Well, we didn't have much time to plan, yesterday, because Sunday, was the last day that the Triple Delta's would be using the Party bus. So we had to go spur of the moment. If we would have had a week to plan, then things would have been smoother. But either way, we still pulled the mass killing off. Hopefully no one spotted the make of our car and your license plate number, Greg."

My eyes got wide, "Wow! I didn't even consider someone seeing my license plate number. Damn!"

Jeremy leaned forward. "Well if someone did write down your license plate number, the police would definitely be able to find out who you are and where you stay. They haven't kicked in your door yet. So I'd said you're home free. For now at least."

I said, "You might be right, Jeremy….anyway, what's up with some Madden? Any of you wanna go at it?"

Richard Picked up one of the controllers, "I'll play you."

As we were playing madden, Richard, Jeremy, and I began talking about assignments that were due in our classes tomorrow. As I was telling Richard about a paper I had to write for English class, there was some running near Jeremy's door and then some loud banging at the door. A voice outside said, "Open up. It's the police."

Jeremy, Richard and I looked at each other with our jaws dropped. We closed our eyes and tried to hold our breathing, while listening to the police outside the door. There were three loud knocks and then the door came swinging open. One of the officers had kicked it in. The police had on bulletproof vests, helmets with clear face protectors, and carried assault rifles. A muscular, white police officer, who led the other five in the room, yelled, "Every last one of you, on the floor now! Put your hands behind your head!"

Richard, Jeremy and I wiggled out of our seats and put our hands behind our heads. The police officers patted us down and a female officer said, "Which one of you is Jeremy Malis?"

Jeremy sighed. "That's me. I'm Jeremy."

The female officer said, "Pat him down and pick him."

A tall, black police officer grabbed me by the arm and helped me get up. "Up on your feet. What's your name?"

Trembling all over, I looked at him. "Greg Rotten."

"Who's your buddy over there? Don't get yourself caught up in something that you had no part of."

I looked at Richard, as a shorter, black cop aggressively assisted him in getting up. "His name is Richard."

The female cop put handcuffs on Jeremy and escorted him out of the room. The tall black cop said, "We need to talk to you guys downtown."

The police escorted Richard and me to the police cars, outside of the dorms. When we arrived at the station, the police separate Richard and me and interrogated us in different rooms. A white detective with glasses walk into the room and put a cup of coffee in front of me, "My name is Officer Hutchens and I am investigating a homicide that took place at the triple Alpha frat house on Saturday. We had a witness identify Jeremy as the killer. Do you know anything? A girl named Sarah was stabbed to death. Did Jeremy mention anything to you?"

I shook my head. "He didn't say anything to me. I have just been playing Madden the whole time with Richard, before you guys came in."

Officer Hutchens asked me lots of questions about Jeremy and the murders. I played dumb and repeated in various different ways that I didn't know anything about the murders and that Jeremy didn't mention anything to me.

Officer Hutchens gave me his card. "Call me if you have any information about this crime."

Officer Hutchens walked me out of the room and I saw Richard waiting in chair outside the door. The officer escorted Richard and me to a police car and drove us back to our dorm. Richard and I got out of the car and walked into the dorm. Richard followed me into my room and sat down at my desk. I locked the door and told Richard that I didn't tell the police anything about Jeremy or the murders. Richard nodded and told me that he played dumb the whole time as well. We both agreed that we needed to stay quiet about the crimes and that we would wait until the police left the dorm, before we discussed anything about Jeremy's arrest. Richard and I watch the continuing news coverage on Sarah's murder. The news channel showed Jeremy's picture and reported him as the main suspect in Sarah's murder. The news also showed reporters waiting at the police station for Jeremy to arrive in a police car. As soon as the car arrived that was holding Jeremy, Reporters rushed in. An officer ushered Jeremy into the police station, reporters following and constantly sticking microphones near Jeremy's mouth and asking questions. Jeremy ignored most of the reporters, except for a skinny, redhead who asked him, "What could a sweet girl like Sarah do that would make you be so cruel?"

Jeremy turned towards the red haired reporter and said, "Lady, you don't know what you're talking about, I'm innocent. Get out my face!"

I shook my head. "Dang, Jeremy. We were supposed to chill out overseas with lots of women. Why did you have to mess everything up, man?"

I looked at my watch. Thirty minutes had gone by. I opened my door and checked the hallway for the police. It seemed the police had completely left the dorm. I locked my door. "We're free to talk now, Richard."

Richard said, "That snitch told on him. You should snitch, Greg. He needs to know what it's like to be snitch on."

"No, he's got dirt on me also. At least he didn't say that you or I took part in it."

"I know, but we can't let things go down like this. That blond sissy boy has to pay for this crap."

I nodded. "Soon. We'll get him. Don't worry."

There was a knock at the door but when I looked through the peephole, there was no one there. I opened the door and looked in the hallway, but I still didn't see anyone. I shut the door and sat down on my bed. "Someone is playing with me, I guess."

I heard two more knocks at my door and yelled, "Who the hell is that? Open the fucking door and come in!"

I looked at Richard and got up to open the door. When I opened the door, someone punched me in the face and I fell to the floor. I looked up at Larry, who walked in the room aiming a pistol at me. Eric and Jake were behind him. Larry sternly said, "Get up on your knees and turn around. Both of you. Look at the windows and don't say a word."

Someone tied up my hands and put duct tape over my mouth from behind. Eric walked over to the window and closed the blinds and curtains. I heard the door lock and Eric turned me around to face Richard as Jake turned Richard around to face me.

Larry pistol whipped Richard. "See what you monkeys have done? I almost went to jail over some stuff that I didn't even have anything to do with!"

Larry turned and slapped me in the mouth with the gun. I shouted, "Oh shit! Damn it! Mother Fucker!" as the impact from the strike knocked spit from my mouth and left me with a pulsating headache."

"My momma knows about this. Everyone on campus knows about this. Everyone was looking at me like I'm the murderer. The only reason that I didn't turn you two monkeys in is because you know what I did to Jessica. I can't take any chances on you having a guilty conscience and turning yourself in. From there, what would keep you from snitching on me? Seeing that I told on your boy. I can't go to prison," Larry hissed.

Larry looked at Eric. "Pass me that knife."

Eric pulled out a machete from under his shirt and handed it to Larry. Larry handed Eric the pistol and took a long, thin piece of wood out of his pocket with a shark tooth attached at the end.

Larry said, "Hold his head."

I mumble, "Wait", as Jake pulls my head back against his leg.

Larry slapped me in the jaw with the toothed club. The shark tooth punctured my skin and the impact knocked out one of my teeth. Larry yanked the shark tooth free from my jaw and walks towards Richard. I groaned loudly as the pain travels through my body. Larry went on to strike Richard. Larry pressed the club so hard against Richard's jaw that the shark tooth broke free. Richard writhed. The duct tape only allowed weak moans to escape.

"Move," Larry told Jake as he grabbed Richard behind the neck. He looked me in the eye. "You see what happens when you screw with me, Greg? People get hurt."

Richard's eyes were watery and he was breathing deeply. Larry slashed Richard across the chest with the machete and blood ran down his shirt. Larry pulled the knife out of Richard's chest and pushed him face first on the ground. Richard moaned violently as Larry continued to stab him in the back. After about a minute of the attack, Richard's moaning died out and Larry looked at me with drops of blood running down his face. "You see what you made me do?"

Larry spat in my face, crawled closer and stabbed me in the stomach. The blade went so deep that it passed out my back, catching Jake in the shin. Jake yelped, "My leg, you idiot! Oh, god!!"

I moaned uncontrollably and started to cry.

Larry yelled, "Jake! I'm sorry, man. I didn't mean! Sit down, man. Let me look at your leg."

I looked down at the growing stain of blood on my shirt and running down my pants. Behind me, Eric and Larry helped Jake sit down on my bed. Larry sternly said, "It's over. We got to get you to a hospital. Let's finish up and get out of here."

Larry flipped Richard over, cut his stomach open, and started pulling his intestines out. "Put the message on the wall, Eric!"

Eric kneelt/kneeled next to Richard's body and started rubbing his hand through Richard's intestines as Larry crawled back over towards me. I moaned hysterically as Larry grabbed my shirt and stabbed me in the chest until I blacked out.

#

Eight

I woke up in a hospital bed, breathing deeply, with tubes in my nose. Wires were tape

over my chest and bandages wrapped all over my stomach and chest. I looked around the room.

A familiar figure, sat in a chair to the right side of my bed, a short, skinny woman with blonde hair. My eyes teared up and a gleaming smile came across my face, "Mom, what happened? How did I get here? How long have I been here?"

I used to call my mom every day when I first arrived at Washington Bay. My mom was one of my best friends. I could talk to her about anything that happened, and I did—except, of course, for the murders and my part in them.. After a couple weeks of hanging out with Richard I called my mom every other day. By October, I was calling my mom every other week.

Now she hugged me and kissed me on the forehead. "I'm glad you're okay and in one piece. You were attacked on campus by a group of serial killers. Had I known that there was a serial walking around on campus, I would have told you that you need to come home for the semester. Or at least we could have seen if you could transfer to another school. But I'm just glad you're alive. The doctor said you were stabbed 8 times in the stomach and chest. Your stomach was cut open. The residential assistant in your dorm was helping someone move in to a room on your floor and notice a trail of blood outside your room. He found you and Richard and called 911. You immediately went to surgery. The doctors said that you lost so much blood that it's a miracle that you're alive. Thank God! When the doctors called me, I booked me a flight and got here as fast as I could."

I half hugged her lightly. The pressing of my mother's body, against my bandaged torso, caused a sharp pain to travel through my body with broken timing. I jerked away from my Mother, "I love you, Mom. Did they catch the guy who stabbed me?"

"No. They got away whoever they were. The police are doing their best to catch them, but no one saw anything. I heard on the news that these killers have murdered a few people on campus. They call themselves the Washington Bay Vampires."

I touched my cheek and felt some stitches on my jaw underneath a bandage. I rubbed the wrapping around my stomach, covering more stitches on my stomach. "Will I have any trouble eating?"

"You'll be mostly on a liquid diet for a while until you fully recover. I'll run and get you a milk shake from McDonalds, if you want."

"Did the doctors have to remove any of my organs? ...Am I missing my intestines?"

My mom squinted at me. "No. The doctors said that you were stabbed multiple times in the stomach and chest, but there was no severe damage to anything internally. The doctors stabled and stitched up your wounds. You're going to feel a lot of pain for a week in your chest and stomach, especially when you're walking and when you go to the bathroom. The doctor gave me your prescription to get your pain medication."

I rubbed my eyes. "How long have I been here? Where is Richard? Is he okay?"

My mom sighed. "You have been here for about a day. You've been asleep for nearly twelve hours after an eight hour surgery."

I put my arm on my mom's shoulder. "Where is Richard? He is alive, right?"

My mom closed her eyes and held my hand. "Richard passed away. I'm sorry."

"Damn it! This can't be fucking happening. That motherfucker! I'm going to get that son of a bitch."

My mom's eyes were watery and she held my hands tightly. "It'll be alright. The police will catch these guys. Do you remember what they look like? Had you ever seen them on campus? Maybe at a party."

I covered my face with my hands. "No. I don't remember what they looked like. I just remember watching the news with Richard and then I woke up in the hospital here."

"Relax. When you start to feel better, maybe you can call Richard's parents and see how they are taking all this in. I think it will help all of ya'll heal from this tragedy and bring ya'll some closure."

"No! No! I don't think I can talk to them. It will pain me even more to hear Richard's love ones suffering and to know that if I was a little more cautious and locked my door, their son would be alive."

"You can't blame yourself for this. You did all you could do. In that same situation, everyone else would have done the same thing. We'll if you are not going to call his parents, are you at least planning to go to his funeral."

"No. I don't think I could bare seeing Richard lying in a casket and to know that my lack of precaution caused his death. It would make me wanna kill myself."

"Don't talk like that Greg! You were a great friend to Richard and this whole event could have happened to anyone. I'm sure he would tell you that if he were alive."

Mom gave me another hug and then we started some small talk about how my family was doing back home and how my classes have been going for the semester. A couple hours went by and then the police came by the hospital to ask me some questions about the guys who attacked me. They asked my mother to leave the room and my mom waited in the lobby. I was insistent that I could not remember what the killers looked like. I told the police that all I could remember was hanging out with Richard in my room, watching television, and then waking up in the hospital. The police left after about twenty minutes of consistently receiving the same answers. My mom reentered the room, about an hour later. I told my mom about what the police had asked me and that they promised me that they would find the people that had attacked me. The doctor came by soon after and told me that after a few day of rest in the hospital, I should be well

enough to leave and go back home.

My mom stayed at the hospital with me for the rest of the day. When it was closed to

midnight, she kissed me on the cheek, gave me some clothes and some money, and told me that

she was going to sleep for the night at a hotel nearby. She would head back home, early in the

morning, because she had to take my grandmother to the hospital for surgery, tomorrow. My

grandmother went to the hospital about a month ago for a regular checkup and they found a lump

on one her breast. After performing a biopsy on some of the tissue from the lump, the lump on

my grandmother's breast turned out to be cancerous and would need to be removed. My

grandmother is supposed to have surgery tomorrow. I kissed my mom on the cheek and told her

farewell.

After a few days went by, I left the hospital and took a cab to my dorm. My cell phone

and wallet were missing from my room. I read the newspaper as the cab driver drove me from

the hospital to my dorm. One of the articles in the newspaper was about the murder and stabbing

that took place in my dorm room. The headline read: *Washington Bay Vampires strike again!* The

article showed a picture of Richard and stated that he was ambitious student, majoring in

Pharmacy and mentioned that no funeral had been scheduled yet, according to their sources. The

article also mentioned me as a friend of Richard's who was stabbed and brutally injured in the

attack. It stated that I was the first victim to survive the attacks by the Washington Bay Vampires.

Meanwhile, the police had trouble connecting the attack to the other attacks by the Washington

Bay Vampires. This attack was different from the other in that both victims had their stomachs

sliced open, but the killers did not slice up the intestines of either. The message left on my wall

was also different from the other messages left by the Washington Bay Vampires: *Washington*

Bay Vampires for Life. All of our messages talked about paying tribute and were more than one line. According to the article, these inconsistencies caused police to suspect there was a copycat on campus. I didn't know whether to smile or frown. People say imitation is next to flattery. In a twisted way, Larry's actions had flattered me, but also insulted me at the same time. Not only was Larry trying to frame us in a manner that showed that he was inspired by our killings, now he was taking our spotlight.

I turned to the next page and read an article on Sarah's murder. Alongside a picture of her, the article stated that Sarah was a positive and cheerful person who was majoring in nursing. The article also showed a picture of Jeremy and stated that Jeremy had been charged with first degree murder and was awaiting trial in prison. The police didn't suspect anyone else was involved in Sarah's murder. The article described Jeremy as a sketchy loner on campus, who had trouble with the law in high school. It also indicated that Jeremy had received psychological treatment for his violent tendencies in the past.

When I got to the dorm, I headed to the residential assistant's office. I was checking out for good and would be getting an apartment near campus. I rented a small U-Haul truck and put all my belonging in storage while I drove around town to find an apartment.

After viewing lots of apartments and filling out lots of applications, I headed to Vulture Trail prison to talk to Jeremy. I signed in and sat in the waiting room until I was able to speak with Jeremy.

I sat down at one of the divided booths, right before, Jeremy sat down and picked up the phone. Jeremy looked like he had just woken up and hadn't eaten in a week, but smiled when he saw me. "What's the word? How are the plans going?"

"You didn't hear?"

"About what? Do the police have a suspect?"

"Nothing about that. About Richard"

"He was arrested?"

"He's dead, man."

Jeremy's eyes widened and his mouth dropped, "What? What happened?"

"Richard was chilling with me in my apartment and some guys came in and killed him. They nearly killed me too. I got stitches, cuts and bruises all over my body."

"You know who these guys are? You see their faces?"

I put my finger over my lip and nodded. "Not on the phone."

"Why not?"

"One of them is someone that you know."

"A friend?"

"No. Someone that you're disgusted with. Recently. Think about it. Who do you think would want us dead?"

"Larry?"

I put my finger over my lip again and nodded.

Jeremy shook his head. "That little trashy snitch. What did you tell the police?"

"I told them that I didn't know who the killers were and check this out—they tried to take our style."

"What do you mean?"

"Check out the newspaper on the story when you can."

"You're not worried that he might come back and try to finish the job?"

"I moved out of the dorm and I'm waiting to hear back from a couple apartment complexes. They haven't talked much about Richard's murder on the news, so maybe Blondie will think I'm dead. Even if he does find out, I'll be off campus, somewhere he doesn't know. Blondie needs to pay for this."

"Don't do anything stupid. You don't want to end up like me. Stuck in a cell. Eating filth three times a day. Fearful of molestation every time you take a shower. I didn't think prison was this hard. It's tough, man."

Jeremy's eyes became watery and he sighed. "My folks have nearly denied me as their son. I talked to my mom once on the phone and she was nearly in tears. My dad was furious and hung up me as I was talking to him. My mom came to visit me once and she couldn't even look me in my face. She said she was embarrassed to call me her son and told me that she didn't want to speak to me till the trial was over. And she said that my dad didn't want to talk to me ever again. That this murder was the last straw. I messed up my life. I told you and Richard that I hated parties."

I closed my eyes and covered my face with my hands. "I'm sorry, man. Maybe I shouldn't have pressured you to go to the party. But I just couldn't see you sitting in the dorm room alone on Homecoming while Richard and I partied. If we didn't go out that day, maybe Richard would still be alive."

My eyes became watery and my breathing deepened.

I shook my head. "Jesus. Richard. Jesus .Jeremy. You guys were my best friends. Even if I do finish our plans, what good is all the money in the world, if I don't have anyone to share it with?"

Jeremy said, "Hold it together. If not for the money or a better life, Greg, carry out our plans for Richard and me. Richard is gone and I'm probably never going to see the light of day again. For all the isolation, bullying, and cruel treatment that we have suffered from our peers on campus, I think that at least one of us deserves a chance at a better lifestyle."

A guard walked in the room and tapped Jeremy on the shoulder. "Your time is up."

I sternly said, "Jeremy, I'm going to get you out of here. Somehow."

Jeremy stood up, nodded and walked out the room alongside the guard. I signed out of the prison and headed to my car.

Angie, the sales agent at Maple Apartments, called my cell phone. I had heard about Maple Apartments from Julie, a sales agent at another apartment complex I'd visited. Julie told me that for the small budget that I had, Maple Apartments would suit me well.

Angie told me a room was available for five hundred dollars a month. I started burning with joy when she told me that the five hundred dollars included all utilities. I just hoped that the apartment wasn't roach infested or near a rough area. I drove to the apartments, which was about fifteen minute commute from campus. The apartment was located in a middle class area. I didn't see any run down houses or shacks, but I didn't see any mansions or three story houses either. The majority of people walking the streets wore work clothes. I didn't see any women with tight miniskirts or guys with sagging pants. Every car that passed looked like a gas saver, although rust spots on the front and rear of most of the vehicles revealed that the cars were at least a few years old. The apartment complex looked fairly new and consisted of at least twenty, two story flats. Each was connected to one other flat and separated from other joined flats by ten feet of yard or by the street, which led from the entrance to an exit on the other side of the complex. I went into the office near the front and filled out the paperwork with Angie.

I called my mom to get the security deposit and first month's rent. She agreed to send me the money after I told her how unsafe it was for me to live in the dorm after being attacked and that there might be a chance the killer would return if he found out I was still alive. I promised my mom that I would get a small job to pay the rent and I would pay her back as soon as possible, the money for the deposit and rent that she gave me. I left the apartment complex to get all my belonging from storage.

After gathering all my belongings in the U-Haul truck, I returned to Maple Apartments. I entered my furnished, one bedroom apartment and began unpacking. The place had crème colored carpeting in the living and dining rooms, which surrounded an open kitchen. The bathroom and bedroom were to the right of the front door and dining room. The walls were painted white and the ceiling was ten feet high. I had an armless couch sitting perpendicular to a love seat and across from a single shelved wooden entertainment set in the living room. There was a wooden table and four wooden chairs in the dining room. The bedroom had a queen size bed and closet doors that rolled open. After unpacking, I grabbed my comforter off my bed and wrapped myself up, cozy, on the couch and started watching more news coverage on Sarah's murder. I shook my head as they degraded Jeremy's image. I turned to Fox, which was showing a show called *Cold Case Files Investigations*. Every episode covered a different cold case file that a police department somewhere in America had solved. The Cold Case File the show was covering that day was about an arsonist who had burned down several buildings in the Miami area and videotaped the burnings from a distance. Miami is about a half hour from my new apartment in Fort Lauderdale. The arsonist would send the videotaped burnings, which he proudly claimed as his own work, to the police department. However, the arsonist never revealed his identity on the videotapes. The police had a hard time figuring out who sent the tapes and most of their leads went cold. The arsonist' signature marking was a ying yang sign dug in the front yard of every building he burned. The videotapes showed that the arsonist taped all the burnings from the same location. The arsonist was never caught and is still at large. The show ended by asking viewers to call the Miami-Dade police department if they had any leads. I turned off the television and lay down on the love couch until I fell asleep. I had a horrible dream that night. I was running with Richard through an alley until we hit a dead end. Richard and I turned around as we heard the sound of someone in the distance run toward us. It was nearly pitch black in the alley, except for the small amount of light scattered by the full moon. The footsteps stopped and in the distance, Richard and I saw two red glowing eyes. I leaned back against the brick wall with my fist balled up. Larry stepped out of the shadows, pointing a pistol at Richard and me. Larry chuckled and then shot Richard in the face. My mouth dropped as I watched Richard fall to his knees and collapse, face first, on the ground. Larry aimed the gun at me and started to smile. I glared at Larry and breathed rapidly. Larry laughed at me and I opened my mouth to scream. As soon as my screaming began, a stream of flame extended from my mouth and lit Larry's body on fire. Larry screamed and rolled around on the floor. I closed my mouth and looked down, smiling, at Larry as he tried to put out the flames. The flames continued to grow as Larry spun around on the floor. As his writhing sent him crashing into me, my clothes caught on fire which started to eat away at my flesh. I fell to the floor and tried to roll about to put out the flames, but they continued to grow. I started to scream as my face remained as the one part of my body that was not devoured by the fire. I woke up sweating and crying for help.

I looked at the Freddy Kruger clock on my living room wall. It was 2am. I went into the bathroom and splashed my face with water from the bathroom sink. After drying off, I began taking deep, slow breaths and looked in the mirror, thinking about blowing a stream of fire into

Larry's face and thinking about how good it felt to torture Larry for all he has done.

I got dressed and drove to Wal-Mart. I bought a gardening hoe, a small axe, a butcher

knife, a hunting knife, a black bed sheet for a twin size mattress, a box of matches, a pair of

black nylon stockings and a two gallon gas can. I stopped at a gas station on the way back and

filled up the can. Back at the apartment I cut head and arm holes in the black sheets to make a

gown. I cut a two foot long piece off the gown to keep the hem from dragging. I cut the foot end

of one nylon stocking off to make a mask and placed it into a bag with the black sheet that I had

made into a gown. I got into my car and drove within a block of the triple Alpha frat house.

I parked within fifty feet of the frat house and cautiously walked up to it. I didn't see any

lights on in the frat house or in any of the houses nearby. I went back to my car and put on the

gown on. I put the nylon mask over my face and got the hunting knife, gardening hoe and gas

can from the trunk. I walked to the front of the frat house, looking around for any witnesses. I

left the hoe and gas can on the lawn and carried the hunting knife to the door. I rung the doorbell

three times and crouched under the peephole. I waited a few minutes and got no answer. I walked

behind the bushes and looked in, through the open blinds, checking if anyone was on the couch. I

crept to the other side of the house and looked for anyone in the dining room. I walked around to

the side and hopped the backyard gate. No lights were on at the back of the frat house, either.

The back door seemed like it wanted to open up when I jiggled the knob, but a weak

padlock kept it from opening. I looked left and then right, before I charged and front stomped the

back door open. I entered, gripping the hunting knife, and walked around, looking for any Alpha

members. I checked the kitchen, the bedrooms, the living room and the dining room for Alpha

members, to no avail. I opened the front door and grabbed the gas tank. I carried it upstairs into one of the bedrooms and began pouring the gas on the floor. Walking backwards from the

bedroom, I poured it over the carpeted wooden floors through the hallway, down the stairs,

through the living room, the kitchen, the dining room and out the front door.

I threw the emptied can on the ground and picked up the hoe from the front lawn. I began

uprooting the grass and scraping at the surface of the dirt while walking in a circle. I kept

scraping until I had made a large circular trench, a few inches deep. From a point on the circle I

made another line across the trenched circle in a letter S pattern. I dug one small hole in each of

the circular ends of the curve. I stood back and smiled at the ying and yang sign.

Digging completed, I threw down the gardening hoe as the neighbor on the left of the

house came out in her night gown with her keys in hand and her brown hair, wrapped in curlers.

"Dear God!" the lady screamed. She ran to her car where it was parked on the street.

I turned in her direction and took the box of matches from my pocket. The lady was

shaking as she quickly opened the door and struggled to turn on the car's ignition, which

squealed for several seconds before stopping and then squealed for several more. The lady

continuously turned the key, back and forth. I watched her struggled from the front lawn. I stared

at the lady and struck a match. I walked over to the front door and tossed the lit match onto the

gasoline-drenched porch. A flame ignited and spread over the threshold and through the house.

I heard the lady's car come on and I turned around to stare at her. The lady glanced at me

with tears in her eyes as she sped off down the street with the reflection of the enflamed house in

her rear view mirror. I turned and picked up the nearly empty gas can. About a third of a cup of

gasoline had dripped down the sides of the can. I poured it in the ying and yang trench, stuck a

match, and dropped it in. Flames burned in the windows on the first and second floor of the frat

house now. Smoke was coming from the front door, the windows, and cracks in the roof. The flame in the trench ate the surrounding grass, but slowly died out as the moisture in the surrounding grass, from the morning watering by the sprinklers and the dry dirt kept the flames from growing. I took off running back to my car as the lights in houses across the street came on. I jumped in my car and sped off, heading across town towards my apartment.

When I got a mile or so from the burning building, I heard lots of police sirens in the far distance. I snatched the mask off my face and threw it in the back seat.

When I got to a red light with no other drivers around, I put the car in brake and took off the gown. I tossed it in the back seat and proceeded to drive home. When I got home, I grabbed the gown and mask from the back seat and brought them in. I stuffed the mask and gown in a suitcase in my closet. I jumped in the shower, constantly washing my hands and smelling them for gasoline.

After I got dressed, I took a screwdriver and went out to my car. I removed my license plates and hid them under the refrigerator. From the fridge I grabbed a can of Bud Lite. I drank it down in twenty seconds and wrapped myself on the love couch with my bed comforter. I tried to sleep for a few hours, jumping up every time I heard a car drive past my apartment. When at last I fell asleep, I had only a few hours to get some shut eye before class started.

#

Nine

I woke up, around noon, and realized that I had overslept my classes for the day. I turned on the television to a news channel. Fox news was covering the burning of the triple Alpha frat house. Police believed the ying and yang arsonist that had burned several buildings in the Miami area, moved to the Washington Bay area and was responsible. I began eating my breakfast, Frosted Flakes cereal, as a witness with long, brown hair spoke about what she had seen the night the house caught on fire. The news had blotted out the witnesses face digitally, but I could still see her hair and profile perfectly. The witness was the next door neighbor that caught me red handed and dashed to her vehicle. I could tell it was her because of her hair and because she became very emotional during the interview and her voice sounded exactly like the fleeing neighbor who screamed, "Dear God!"

The lady said that she saw a short, skinny male dressed in an all-black gown and wearing a black mask over his face. The news showed interviews with Triple Alpha members. I smiled as some of the triple Alpha members displayed their disgust for my handiwork, verbally with lots of anger and lots of gnashing of their teeth. The news reporter said that police suspected that the arsonist may be a member of triple Alpha or someone that knew triple Alpha members in some way. I started chucking hysterically as the reporters interviewed Larry. Larry's eyes were watery and his face was red as the reporters asked him how he felt about the tragedy.

Shaking nervously, Larry said, "I just hope that the police find out who did this and bring him to justice. Last week, we had a murder at one of our parties, which already brought a lot of grief to our organization and now some monster burned down our building. We had a lot of memories in that house and for someone to just burn our home down for fun or for some twisted reason is just plain cold and ugly. There is nothing that we could have done to deserve this. But at least the memories that my frat brothers and I shared in will live in our hearts forever. And no one, not the monster that burned down our house, not anyone will be able to take those memories from us".

A tear dropped from Larry's right eye and he stared into the camera. "Whoever you are, please turn yourself in. And if any of you out there know who this monster is, please do the right thing and turn him in. Whoever you are, you creep, we're going to find you and you're going to rot for a long time in a cell!"

I changed the channel and watched *Titanic* on HBO. I looked through the blinds to see if anyone was near my apartment. I didn't see anyone outside near my car, so I grabbed my license plates from under the refrigerator and screwed them back on. I spent the rest of the afternoon searching the Internet for part time jobs in the area. I wrote down a list of jobs I thought were easy to get and would be the most flexible—cashier jobs, pizza delivery and fast food jobs. I drove around town and applied at several of stores that were on my list. Most said that they already hired someone else or that they would call me. But at last a manager named Thomas, who worked at Dave's Pizza's, hired me on the spot as a delivery driver. I called my mom, told her that I had landed a job and that I would pay her back her money soon. Of course she insisted that I didn't have to pay her back, but I told her that I wanted to anyway.

#

Later that night, I ran a Google search on Rachel Williams. I was trying to see if I could find the location of her apartment. Random web sites with people who had similar names kept popping up. I went on Facebook, but the site blocked me from viewing her page because she had made it private from everyone except her friends. I had a few friend requests in my inbox, including one from Larry. He had also left me an email.

All Larry said in the email was *how are you?*

I accepted the request so that I could look on Larry's page for any information on Rachel.

One of his status updates said, "*Looking forward to watching Rachel mud wrestle with Jessica Ambers at the swim meet on Saturday*!"

I logged out and went to the Washington Bay college website. I went to the sports link and saw the schedule for the swim meets this fall. Washington Bay had a swim meet across town against a community college called James Peters on Saturday. I searched for the address of James Peters community college and wrote it down on a sheet of paper. Computer research done for the day, I went into the living room to watch some television. HBO had another good movie this time, named *American Pie 2*. The movie was about a group of old high school students, coming back home for the summer after a year of college. There was a scene near the end where the group of boys discussed their struggles with adapting to life after high school. One of main characters said, "What's most important is that we stay in touch with one another and continue to always be friends", and then I covered my eyes with one hand and punched the love couch with the other.

I lowered my hand from my face and shook my head, "Jeremy." I took a deep breath. "Richard. How could I let this happen?"

I turned the channel to a gangster film on TCM. There was a scene where a gangster named Tony found out that Jimmy, one of his gang members, had given information to the police about a robbery. The information was incriminating enough that it landed Tony's best friend, Eddie, in Jail. Tony accused Jimmy of snitching and Jimmy denied it. Tony plays a recording of Jimmy ratting on him. Jimmy begged for his life and Tony laughed as he emptied a round of bullets from a tommy gun into Jimmy. I smiled the whole time that Tony was shooting Jimmy. Snitches get stitches!

I laid back and fell into a daydream. I pictured myself as gangster who had just robbed a bank and hung out at my place with a couple of my goons, Larry, Eric, and Jake. In the dream, as I drunk rum and talked with my friends, the ameche rang.

I pick the ameche off the hook, "It's Greg."

"Greg, It's Jeremy. I'm in stir. The coppers found an illegal bean shooter and some of the bent ice that we glommed from the jewelry store in my boiler, as we were heading back to the hide out."

"Christ! How did the coppers know about the heist and know what kind of car you were in to pull you over? We planned this thing out for a while. There should have been no alarms, no witnesses near that alley, and no employees on site. There must be a stool pigeon, among us. Maybe that new can opener that you brought with you."

"I doubt it was John. He is in here, but Eric, Larry and Jake are missing. They left in a separate bucket. I bet one of them have been peaching to coppers. The gum-shoe knew exactly where to find the diamonds, in a small department, built into the passenger side door. When you get a chance, send someone to bail me and John out. There are a few grifters in here from another gang. I think they might bump me."

"Okay, I'll send my moll down there to get you guys out of the big house, right after I put these snitches in Chicago overcoats. I'll talk to you soon. I have to take care of some business first."

I hung up the phone, frowning, and Larry approached me with a bottle. "Bad news? You'll take it better with a little more rum…..if you need me and chopper squad to handle a few guys, just give me the word"

I took the bottle from Larry and broke it over his head. "You dirty rats. You snitched on Jeremy. I should fill all of you with lead!"

Larry held his bloody forehead with one hand and raised his other hand high in the air. "Please, Greg. We didn't do anything. I would never tell on you. You got to believe me! A bull must have saw Jeremy leaving the jewelry store and informed the police on his whereabouts."

I walked over to the closet and pulled out a Tommy gun from the shelf. Eric and Jake put both their hands up.

Eric fell to his knees and his eyes got watery. "Come on, Greg. How long have we been friends? Why would I want to turn you in to the cops?"

I aimed the Tommy gun at Eric. "Jeremy said that the pigs knew where to find where he had stashed the ice. The only way that they would have known where to find the diamonds is if someone within our operation told the police where to find them. You guys saw Jeremy hide the diamonds and oddly they caught John and Jeremy,…… but they didn't catch any of you. . My only question to you all is why you did it. Were you jealous of Jeremy? Maybe he didn't give you in a share in the money. Or maybe you all are trying to find a way to take control of the mob. And where is Richard? He never was one to miss out on drinking time with his buddies. Well, where is he?"

Jake, Eric and Larry shrugged their shoulders and looked at each other.

I nodded. "I see. Maybe you want to do me the same way. Maybe that's why all of you showed up in the first place. To get me drunk enough where I couldn't defend myself, and then all of you would fill me with lead. Not going to happen like that."

I gripped the Tommy gun with both hands. "Put aside a glass of rum for me while you're at the after party with Jesus."

I chuckled as I unloaded twenty rounds into Larry's chest and then put twenty rounds into Eric's stomach as he pleaded on his knees. Jake ran for the door and I emptied the clip into his back.

The Tommy gun started to click and I tossed it on the floor. "Party poopers."

I lit a cigar and put it in mouth as my vision became blurry.

I shook my head and came out of my daydream, still muttering, "No witnesses. No case."

I turned the television off and took a hot shower.

#

After a few days had passed, I drove to visit Jeremy at Vulture Prison. I had to be at work soon after, so at that time I could only talk to Jeremy for a half hour. Jeremy sat down at the conference booth with me and picked up the phone. He had let all his facial hair grow out and looked like he had just woken up, with sleep in his eyes, his orange jacket wrinkled and his hair unkempt.

I picked up the phone. "Trouble sleeping?"

"One of the inmates tried to escape last night, everyone was hollering and making all this noise, while the prison alarm went off for hours. I couldn't sleep through all that mess. So, how are the plans going?"

"Better than expected. I'm going to take care of the next one Saturday. Tomorrow, I'm going to find out where she stays and deliver her the gift that she deserves."

"Dang. I wish I could be out there with you. You shouldn't have to do all the work yourself. If I hadn't been so careless and stupid... I should have waited to go out with Lisa that night, like I had originally planned."

"For all you know, Lisa could have stood you up and who knows, maybe you would have met up with Richard and I at the party and the same thing could have happened. Has Lisa come up here to see you?"

"Now that you mention her, no. That selfish whore. After all I have invested in her, this is how she treats me. I've wrote to her every day that I have been in here and she has not written me since nor come to see me. Maybe I creeped her out somehow. Forget her. You can have her."

"Just be patient, maybe after she reevaluates things then she'll come and see you. The way you described her makes her seem worth the chase. But like I said, if you don't want her, I'll take her. Just joking," I said, as I cringed in my seat.

"You can have her. Sorry tramp. I hope the next guy she dates kills her. Maybe if I wasn't thinking about her the whole night, and maybe if I wasn't pissed off because she didn't call me to go out, maybe I wouldn't have….."

"It's in the past now. Whatever was going to happen? Was going to happen. That could have happened to any of us. Every male on campus knows how much of a tease some women can be. Anyway, I figured a way to get you out of here."

"No prison breaks. It's nearly impossible; they caught the inmate that escaped this morning. It will just get me more time and get you put in here with me."

"No. A better way. I can't go into detail because of obvious reasons. But let's just say that the people making these claims against you are about to have a change of heart. No evidence. No witness. No accusers. No case. Then you're free."

"Don't be stupid, man. I appreciate the gesture. But I'm sure Richard would agree that you could do us better on the outside"

"You'll see. Just wait. Soon. Did you see what happen to blond boy's house?"

"Sure."

I pointed at myself and nodded.

Jeremy sighed. "You. Don't let Blondie mess up everything we put together. He probably suspects that it was you. Has he seen you lately?"

"No. But I know he knows that I'm still alive."

"He's going to try and kill you."

"Unless I play it smart."

I looked at my watch. "I got to go. Stay strong Jeremy, it's only a matter of time before you're out here."

I drove to Wal-Mart and bought two thin steak knives. Back home, I searched the backyard of my apartment for a stick. A tree had dropped several dead branches on the ground. I picked up a branch about an inch in diameter and that was nearly decayed all the way through. I took the knives and the decayed branch into the kitchen. I stabbed the branch hard enough so that the tip of the knives went through. I put it on the floor and held it still with one foot as I pushed the steak knife through. I grabbed the handles on the steak knife and bent them back, breaking off the handle. I grabbed both ends of the branch and broke them off. Now the branch was only a few inches long, the middle portion pierced by the knives. I grabbed the handmade fangs off the floor and put them in a suitcase, which I then carried out to the trunk of my car. I brushed the wood particles off my hands, put my work clothes in the back seat, and jumped in to drive to the gun shop a few blocks from Dave's Pizza's.

I walked into Joe's Gun Shop and began looking at the used pistols that they had for sale. I had just a little bit over three hundred left in my bank account after paying rent and my security deposit. Most of the guns were beyond my budget, with the exception of a blue finished nine millimeter for two hundred and twenty bucks and a blue finished Ruger for two hundred. Either would do the job that I had planned well, although I had heard more hype surrounding the nine millimeter than the Ruger. That is, more rappers referenced the nine millimeter than the Ruger. It could be that the word millimeter rhymes with more words than ruger, or most rappers find the nine millimeter the best bang for your buck.

The customer service representative let me hold both guns. I loved the longer barrel on the nine millimeter more than the shorter Ruger. A longer barrel made the gun seem more intimidating. However, the nine millimeter weighed more than the Ruger. I assumed that the extra weight plus the kick back from the gun meant that I would have a hard time aiming, so I bought the Ruger.

The customer service rep told me I would have to wait forty four hours and clear a background check before I could take the gun home. I filled out the background paperwork and promised to be back in two days to pick up the gun. I jumped in my car and headed to work.

#

I loved my delivery job, but hated my boss, Dave. Dave looked like a busted up Santa Claus: a big pot belly, a long white beard, a round nose and thick glasses. He would constantly yell at me for late deliveries. He would constantly frown at me as he would catch me daydreaming, often, mostly, as I put the pizzas into my delivery bag. I often imagined what I could have done to prevent Richard's death. However, I had a really hard time staying on task that night. My nerves were bad, I was filled with guilt for Richard's death, and I was constantly meditating on how to follow and kill Rachel without running into Larry.

I walked in the store after a delivery and the phone rang.

Dave answered the phone, "Dave's Pizza, the number one pizza place in town. We have a special running, two medium pizzas for five dollars each….okay…When did you purchase the pizza?...What type of pizza was it?…I'm sorry to hear that.. What's your name?....Come by in about thirty minutes and I'll have a new pizza ready for you…sorry again."

Dave slammed the phone down, "Greg, come here!"

I walked up to Dave with my hands in my pocket, "What's wrong?"

"What's fucking wrong is a lady just called here complaining that her pizza was cold. What the hell are you doing when you are supposed to make your deliveries? Are you taking twenty minute breaks at your apartment to jerk off? Now we have to make this lady another pizza and the cost for it is coming straight out of my pocket. You keep fucking up like this and you are going to be fired!"

"I'm sorry, Dave. I got a bit lost and the traffic was crazy. There were a few accidents on the road that slowed down my commute to make my deliveries."

 Dave could go screw himself. That fake Santa Claus probably had everything handed to him as a kid. Dave probably never had to work for anyone. Must be nice to make a living bossing people around while they're sweating behind an oven and delivering pizzas. Dave usually came in for a few hours in the morning and then a few hours at night to check on his store.

I suspected that Dave was a pervert. Over even the small amount of time that I spent at the pizza shop, I noticed that he paid the females that worked there more money. Dave didn't allow anyone to go to the bathroom with letting him know, he would follow his female workers to the bathroom whenever they alerted him that they needed a break. Whenever a girl questioned him about following her, he would tell her he wanted to make sure that they were not wasting his paid time, playing in the bathroom. Last week, one of the female employees, Jennifer, quit. When I saw Jennifer on campus a few days later, she told me that Dave tried to look under the bathroom stall while she was taking a pee. When Jennifer confronted him about it, he told her that he heard a scream in the bathroom and was checking on her. Jennifer said that Dave had a creepy look in his eye as she confronted him and she'd felt so uncomfortable that she quit.

After my shift was over at Dave's Pizzas, I headed home to take a shower and go to sleep.

#

I woke up early the next day to get ready for the swim meet at James Peter's at 11. By the time I arrived, his community college parking lot was full of cars and lots of people. I walked slowly into the athletic building near the rear of the college and next to the baseball field. As I walked, I looked around the area for Larry or Rachel. The athletic building had two swimming pools, each a hundred meters in length and fifty meter in width that sat next to one another. There was a long and wide walkway that split the two pools apart and allowed spectators to walk from the entrance to the bleachers on the other side of the building. The athlete's bleachers were opposite the spectators', near the entrance. Some athletes were warming up along the benches, while several of their teammates approached the diving boards for the next race. The bleachers for spectators were nearly full. I made my way up to the top where I saw an empty seat. People cheered for the athletes on the diving boards. I looked around for Larry as the announcer proclaimed the start of the two hundred meter freestyle. I looked over at a blonde girl's shoulder at the guide for the events she held, searching for Rachel's name. I looked closer at the Blonde girl's face and realized that she was Lisa. The same Lisa that Jeremy was interested in. I looked away before Lisa caught me examining her face. Lisa glanced down at the swimmers near the pool and I eyed the guide in her hands. Rachel would race in the four hundred meter freestyle, which was the next event. I looked across the room and saw Rachel stretching with a teammate.

Lisa tapped me on the right arm with the guide. "Here, you take it. You can look at it".

"Thanks. I came to watch one of my friends compete."

"What is your friend's name?"

"Rachel Williams. I met her at a party once and I really made a connection with her."

"Well. You know. She's dating Larry."

"Yes. I know. I'm good friends with Larry, too. I've hung out with him at his frat parties. I feel sorry for what happen to the triple Alpha frat house. First there's a murder and then the place gets burned down. That house was cursed. So what's your name? Who did you come to see?"

"I'm a friend of Rachel and Larry, also. I'm Lisa. I promised Rachel that I would come to see her at the meet. Larry should be here any minute. He never misses any of Rachel's meets."

Lisa had a thin waist, freckles, big breasts, and baby blue eyes. Although some people might find someone with a big nose unattractive. Lisa's long and wide nose made her seem more appealing, especially to me. Her nose made an angelic face woman seem a little bit more down to earth.

"Oh. Lisa. Is your last name Jones?"

"How did you know?"

"You just seem like a Jones."

"Yeah, sure."

"Don't you think that Larry and Rachel make a perfect couple? Larry is president of the triple Alpha frat and Rachel is captain of the swim team."

"You know, she broke a state record. She might go to the Olympics"

"I read about it. Poor Rachel. What a tragedy."

"What do you mean by that?"

"I just meant that it's a tragedy that with all this stress of going to the Olympics, now Rachel has the heavy task of holding Larry together while he grieves over the loss of his frat house."

I held out my hand, "By the way, the name is Greg. So what are you up to tonight?"

"I'm going to a party tonight at my friend Megan's house. It's in the same apartment complex that Larry and Rachel live in."

"Really. Larry and Rachel live right by Megan?"

"Yeah. In fact, Rachel and Larry live in the apartment right above Megan's apartment. If you want, you should come to the party tonight."

"I would like that. Do you have the address?"

Lisa pulled a flyer out of her pants pocket. "Yeah. I have it right here. You can have this, I have another one at my apartment. I stay pretty close to campus."

I put it in my pants pocket. "Cool. Maybe I'll come by after I get off work."

"Where do you work?"

"Dave's Pizza."

"Dave's Pizza! I used to work there a few months ago. I had to leave. The owner came on to me and creeped me out a bit. I don't even like to think about him. You know he has a pending rape charge against him? This girl named Karrie that I used to work there with told me that he tried to force himself on her in the bathroom. Her parents called the cops on him, but Karrie didn't want to press charges. The district attorney is still deciding if they want to go through and press charges on him. It must suck to be working for him."

"The guy is a lazy pig. Sits in his office and won't lift a finger to help me with crap. I'll be glad on the day that I quit that job. So where do you work now?"

"I work in the school cafeteria as a dishwasher. I don't make as much as I did at Dave's Pizzas, but at least the people that I work with are pretty cool."

"Nothing wrong with that. It's like they say, it's the people that you work with that make a job great. Or bad. So who did you come here with? Your boyfriend? Just a friend? Am I in his seat?"

"I came alone. None of my friends wanted to wake up this early on a Saturday to see a swim meet. I usually get up early on the weekends. After a semester of getting up early for a seven o' clock biology class, I have a hard time sleeping past nine."

"Maybe you'll sleep later tomorrow morning. Seeing that you'll probably be out late at the party tonight."

"I doubt it. When I'm even partially intoxicated, I have several sessions of broken sleep."

I gazed at Lisa's big breasts "Since you won't be able to sleep much after partying tonight, maybe we can chill out with some friends at my place."

"We'll see. I'll have to see what my friends have planned afterwards."

I take out my cell phone, "Give me your number. That way, if there's a change in plans, I can call you and let you know."

"555-333-2763 and it's Lisa. If you forgot."

"So what do you have planned after the meet?"

"Probably hanging out with Rachel and Larry. Here comes Larry now. Coming down the aisle behind Jake and Eric."

I leaned over and looked to my right. Eric, Jake and Larry were walking down the bleacher aisle from the opposite side that Lisa and I were sitting in. They were too caught up in excusing themselves as they moved past the seated people in the aisle to notice me.

I leaned toward Lisa and said, "I got to go. I forgot that I have to mail a letter to my mother, I want to send it next day express. So I probably need to get to the post office before 1pm. It was nice meeting you, and hopefully I'll see you at the party tonight."

"The meet is almost over. About thirty more minutes and the teams will be packing up to leave. But alright. See you later."

I covered the right side of my face with my right hand as I walked down the bleacher stairs. Once I was out of the athletic building, I ran to my car.

I drove to the address on the flyer and parked in a space across from the Rachel's apartment building. I parked with the rear of my car facing the apartment building. I leaned the seat back and listened to the radio, keeping an eye on the clock.

An hour went by and there was no sign of Rachel or Larry.

I nodded off for about thirty and woke up to a roaring engine coming into the long parking lot. I turned my music down and looked up into my rear view mirror. A green convertible had pulled into a space right in front of the apartment building where Larry stayed. The driver's side door popped open and Larry stepped out. Larry took a cigarette out and smoked the cigarette. I pulled the hunting knife out of my pocket and let it rest against my stomach. Rachel opened the passenger side door and got out of the car with a duffle bag, then pulled her seat forward to let out Jake, Eric and two females wearing gray sweat pants and gray sweat shirts. When I saw all the people get out of the back seat, I put my hunting knife back in my pocket. The two females were probably on Rachel's swim team. Rachel and the crew had some light conversation while standing outside their car for a few minutes and then proceeded to their

apartment building. I saw them go up one flight of steps and enter their apartment. I got out the

car and snuck towards the apartment building. I slowly walked up one flight of steps, knelt down

on the top step and glanced at the numbers on Larry's front door. I took a pen out of my pocket

and wrote the number on my hand. I slowly walked down the flight of stairs and ran to my car. I

turned my car on and sped out of the apartment complex.

When I got home, I laid down on my couch, until my knees stopped buckling. After the

few hours that it took for my knees to relax, I sent a text to Lisa to tell her that I wasn't going to

be able to attend the party tonight. I told her that I had family in town, but they would be leaving

early in the morning. I added that if she was up to it, we could go get some breakfast early in the

morning after my family left. Lisa said that she would see how tired she was after the party.

I checked my email and found a notification from Facebook saying that Larry had sent

me a message. I went to my inbox on Facebook. Larry's message said, *Thanks for accepting my

friend request, sucks to know that you are still alive.*

I logged off and returned to my couch to watch television. HBO was showing a gangster

film, Scarface. There was a scene in the movie where Tony Montana is supposed to put a bomb

underneath a politician's car to keep him from attended a conference on the war on drugs. It was

my first time watching Scarface, and I was really getting into the movie. The whole time Tony

struggles to press the detonator on the bomb, I was envisioning what would happen to the car.

The doors would probably shoot up in the air; the body would probably flip over and catch on

fire. Cool Beans! Unfortunately, Tony didn't have the heart to press the detonator because there

was a kid in the car with the politician. Just my luck! It would have been cool to see what would

have happen to the kid and his dad. Pieces of their burning carcasses would probably be everywhere, but by looking at the quality of the movie, the technology and the special effects at that time wasn't good enough to put together a gory scene of that caliber. It would be even cooler to see that type of car explosion in real life. I turned off the television, still daydreaming about what a car explosion with people inside would look like.

I headed for my car, drove to Wal-Mart and bought a two gallon gas can. After I filled the gas can up at the Shell gas station nearby, I put the gas canister in my back seat and drove home.

There was a South Park marathon on one of the cable channels, so I sat on the couch and watched television until I fell asleep.

I woke up about nine o' clock that night, jumped in my car and drove to Larry's apartment complex. I parked in the same space that I parked in the first time I visited the complex. The parking lot was filled with cars. Students were standing around in groups on the lawn in front of Larry's apartment building, talking and drinking. I waited in my car for a few hours, listening to music. The people at the party were laughing so loud and so drunk that they never noticed me parking. At midnight, most of the people that were outside had left the apartment complex or went into Megan's apartment to party.

I got out of the car and walked around the area to see if anyone was outside loitering. My check for people came to nothing. I smiled as I spotted Larry's green convertible in front of his apartment building. I walked back to my car and grabbed the two gallon canister of gasoline from out of the back seat. I tip toed over to Larry's convertible and poured gasoline on it, as I ambled around it. I poured half of the can on Larry's car and then proceeded to pour gas on the hoods of all ten cars parked in front of Larry's building. After pouring gasoline on the last car, I ran back to my car and pulled out, stopping in front of Larry's car. I lit a match and threw it out the window at the green convertible. Flames spread over it in the blink of an eye. I sped off as the flames began to spread to the other cars. The temptation to witness Larry's reaction to the fire overpowered me and I stopped in front of another building in the apartment complex, about two hundred feet to the left of Larry's apartment building. I parked with the rear of my car facing Rachel's apartment building. I watched the cars being consumed by flames as students ran out from Megan's apartment to see the disaster. Larry came running around from the back of his apartment building with Jake and Eric screaming. "Who did that to my car, man?"

Residents from the other apartment building crowded outside to see the cars burning. Some residents hooked up garden hoses to outside faucets, along the building and sprayed the flames. The showering on the fire had little effect on the conflagration. The tires on Larry's car exploded and the crowd ran for cover.

Ten minutes passed before I heard the sirens from a fire truck. Drat! No explosion. The fire department put out the fire before it was able to ignite the gas tank on any one of the vehicles. As the residents headed back inside their homes, I headed back to my apartment for the night.

#

Ten

The next afternoon, I drove to Joe's Gun Shop and bought a case of bullets. I signed off

on the paperwork on my gun purchase and picked up the Ruger that I had bought two days ago. I

put it in its box in my trunk and made my way home.

On the way back, I stopped at a gas station and bought a six pack of bottled Miller Lite. I

drove to a park about a mile from my apartment. I took the Ruger, the box of bullets and the six

pack to an open area in the trees. There were several picnic tables scattered throughout the area. I

was the only person at that time visiting. I took five beer bottles and lined them up across a

picnic table under a large oak tree. I sat down at a picnic table about ten feet away. I loaded the

clip with bullets and placed it into the Ruger. First I guzzled down the last bottle of Miller Lite. I

tossed it down, stood and aimed the Ruger at the bottles lined up across a picnic table. I began

emptying the clip on the beer bottles. I would shoot rounds until each bottle engulfed a bullet and

crumbled down into jagged and shiny pieces of glass, before moving on to the next. I was only

able to shoot two bottles before I emptied the clip. My shooting was terrible! I reloaded the clip

and tried to shoot the rest. I had to reload twice before I was able to shoot every last bottle that I

had lined up across the picnic table. I grabbed the box of bullets along with my Ruger and

headed back to my car. The sun had just gone down when I left the forest.

I went home to eat and began watching television to calm my nerves before preparing for

my plans for the night. I smiled as I watched the news coverage focused on the burning of the

cars in Larry's apartment complex. My smile quickly turned to a frown as I flicked through several news channels in search of coverage on the murders done by the Washington Bay

Vampires, to no avail. We needed to get back out there.

After a few hours had passed, I drove to Larry's apartment complex and parked a few

spaces past where I had parked when I lit Larry's car on fire. I waited in the car, taking mental

notes every time a police car drove through the apartment complex. I took mental note of all the

people who left or came home and I took mental note of what apartment that those same people

had left out of.

Three hours had gone by. Each apartment had a patio. Larry's balcony and the balconies

belonging to the people that lived above and below him were on the front of the apartment

building. All three apartments had blinds blocking the view through the glass patio doors, but I

could see the living room lights through the blinds in Larry's place one other apartment on the

third floor, across from Rachel's apartment. I put the black gown over my head and the black

mask in my pocket. The hunting knife went in my left pocket and the homemade fangs in my

back pocket. I held the Ruger in my right hand and got out of the car. I slowly walked up the

stairs to Larry's door and began knocking with my left hand. As I thought of him on the other

side of the door, my hand tightened on the handle on the Ruger. I heard someone walk up to the

door and my knees began to buckle. "Larry?"

Rachel said, "Who is it?"

"It's Greg. I'm a friend of Larry's. I drink beer with his frat brothers."

Rachel opened the door, squinting. "Greg? Oh, I remember. What do you want? Larry is

out with his friends. Did you call him and tell him that you were coming?"

"Naw, Naw. I wasn't stopping by to hang out. I forget my notebook in here the other day,

when I was studying with him for a test."

"Oh. What class?"

"English. He said he could help me with my writing."

"I usually help Larry with his writing. Anyway, you'll have to call him to get your notebook back; he doesn't like anyone coming by unannounced."

Rachel tried to shut the door and I stuck my foot in. Rachel jumped back and I pulled the Ruger out of my pocket. I aimed at Rachel and pushed the door open. I walk into the apartment, shut the door and locked it. Rachel put her hands up and started crying. "Please, take what you want."

I motioned with the gun for Rachel to sit on the couch. "Where are Jake and Eric?"

"They're out with Larry. They're going to come back here later with him."

"Where do they live?"

"I don't know. Those are Larry's friends."

I aimed the Ruger at Rachel's thigh. "Maybe you'll know after a shot in the leg. On the count of three. One. Two."

"Okay. Jake lives in this same apartment complex, in number 312."

"And Eric?"

"I don't know. It's far across town. Please. Just let me go."

I started to lower the gun. "I'm not going to kill you."

Seeing someone in tears just touched an innocent part in me and put me in a mood to extend mercy. Rachel lowered her hands, only to kick the gun out of my hands and reach under the couch to pull out a small knife. I jumped to the floor to get the gun. Securing it, I rolled over to shoot Rachel. I fired the gun and it clicked. I had forgotten to reload after I had left the forest. Rachel dashed towards me with the knife and I took out the six inch hunting knife from my pocket. Getting to one knee, I took a swipe at Rachel's leg as she came towards me, screaming. The blade cut through Rachel's shin, right below the knee, halfway to the bone. Rachel fell to the ground, screeching, and I made a downward strike onto her neck with the blade as she hit the floor. The screaming turned into gurgling sounds and Rachel's body started to shake/writhe violently. I sat beside Rachel as blood flowed from her neck and formed a large pool around her head and shoulders. Rachel's shin bone was poking out of her skin. Eyelids fluttering, Rachel slowly reached out towards me and her lips were moving as if she wanted to tell me something. "Sleep, Rachel, sleep." I began brushing Rachel's hair back until she finally passed away.

I closed Rachel's eyes and took out the fangs from my back pocket. I pierced her neck with the fangs, turned her over on her back and sliced open her belly. I pulled her small and large intestines out and cut them from her body. I chopped up Rachel's intestines and tossed the pieces around Larry's living room. I cut off Rachel's ear and dipped it in the blood inside Rachel's abdomen. I wrote a message on Larry's living room wall with the ear. The message that I wrote read:

All must pay tribute to the Washington Bay Vampires, we don't want you money, we don't want your fame, we want your blood, everyone beware, and the Washington Bay Vampires are back on the prowl, who will be next?

I looked out the blinds to see if anyone was outside walking. There was an old man walking his dog. I waited until he was a far distance away from the apartment building before leaving. I ran to my car and threw the knife, gun and fangs in the front seat. I sped off for home.

Back in my apartment, I put the gun, the knife, the black gown and the fangs in the suitcase in my closet. I wrapped myself up in my covers on my love couch as I flicked through the news channel for any breaking news on the murder. I grabbed a beer out the fridge, guzzled it down and fell asleep.

#

The television was still on when I work up. WKRN was covering Rachel's murder. The news reporter said that the police found D. N. A. evidence at the scene on a knife that Rachel was holding. At a press conference, the police asked for anyone that had any information on the murder to come forward. I turned off the television and began to check the skin on my arms and hands for any cuts. I saw a small cut on the bicep of my left arm, half an inch long and nearly paper thin. I went to the bathroom to clean the cut and put a band aid over it. I got dressed and drove to Wal-Mart.

At Wal-Mart, I bought two pieces of rope, each ten feet long. I put both pieces in my trunk and drove home.

After arriving home and getting comfy on the couch, I sent a text message to Lisa that said, *Are you free this afternoon?*

Lisa called me back. "Greg. I thought that you forgot all about me! You didn't call me that night like you said you would."

"I just been a little busy with school, but trust me, you've crossed my mind several times since then. I'm heading to Wendy's to get me a burger. I want you to come get some food with me. We can talk about what's been happening on campus lately. With all the murders and stuff."

"Cool? I guess? What a weird get together this will be! Why don't we go to the one next to the mall? I wanted to stop later on. That way I can take care of two things at once."

"See you there." I hung up with a smile.

I drove to the mall and walked to the food court. Lisa had arrived before me and was sitting at a table, eating some fries. One my way to get in line at the Wendy's concession stand, I called to her, "the fries taste fresh?"

Lisa nodded. "You can have some of mine if you like, and I'm not going to eat all of this. It'll make me feel fat afterwards."

I stepped out of line and sat down with Lisa to finish off her fries. "I'll get me a number one later."

"You can get it now; don't let me keep from enjoying your meal. If you're hungry, eat."

"My appetite isn't that big right now, I just wanted a little snack. Later on, I'll be hungry enough for a number one and since you offer… This is fine."

"One more week until Thanksgiving break. You going home for the holidays?"

"My home is here. My parents live in Boca Raton, about thirty minutes from here."

"Really? It seems that most of the people at our college come from a different state. Good thing about going to school close to where your family stays is if you ever get homesick, your folks are right down the road."

"And the fact that you don't have to pay for an expensive plane ticket to fly home. I overheard a guy from my English class say that he was going to California for the break. The cost of that ticket, right before the break, my Goodness! Might as well be planning a trip to an exotic island."

"It must be nice to travel, though. I have never been anywhere outside of Florida. The furthest I've traveled was to Tallahassee. A few hours from Georgia's state line."

"It would be nice to travel anywhere outside of this city with all the murders that have happened lately. It makes it hard to sleep at night. It's so sad what happened to Rachel."

"What happened to her? Is she okay?"

"It was on the news. Rachel is dead."

Lisa covered her mouth with her hand and her eyes got watery. Her chest rose and fell with deep, harsh breaths. I took Lisa's free hand. "She was murdered last night. The police are looking for suspects right now."

"Why would someone? There is no reason. Rachel had love for everyone. All she wanted to do was inspire people in a positive way. Was it Larry?"

"The Vampires. They left their signature on her wall. I feel so bad for you. I hate to bring you bad news on our outing. But as a dear friend of Rachel, I think better you heard it from me than from the news."

"I'm even more hurt that no one called me after the news to tell me. Not even Larry. You talk to Larry?"

"Not lately, but I'll talk to him soon and see how he's feeling about everything. Goodness! First Jeremy goes to jail, my friend Richard gets killed, my life was nearly taken from me and now Rachel is dead."

Lisa stared at me for a second and then looked at the ground. "I don't talk to him anymore. You're a friend of Jeremy's. That's how you knew my last name. You've been stalking me. I don't want to talk to you anymore."

Lisa frowned, snatched her hand away from me, wiped it with a paper napkin and began putting on her coat. I showed my palms to Lisa. "No. I don't know Jeremy like that. I'm not his friend. I know of him. He's been on the news a lot and I lived in the same dorm with him. I overheard him talking about dating a girl named Lisa Jones in the laundry room one day. He was very descriptive about you. I just assumed you two were very close. I'm sorry. I didn't mean scare

you or stir up any negative emotions. Please sit down. I won't bring him up again."

Lisa sighed and sat back down. "Jeremy is crazy. Even when I first met him, I just felt

uneasy around him. He would stare at you for a minute before opening his mouth to say

something and every few moments out of the corner of my eye, I could see him ogling at me like

in a trance. I know some people don't have strong social skills, so I knew it was wrong for me to

judge or label Jeremy as a weirdo without really knowing him or his background. Although he

was a little weird, he seemed pretty harmless. He asked me several times to go out with him and

I tried to find reasons why I couldn't go out with him that I could say without hurting his

feelings, but he was persistent , so one day out of the kindness of my heart, I decided to give him

a try."

"How did it go?"

"Actually, Jeremy turned out to be a very good listener. We even became friends. At the

time, I was dating a few other guys and Jeremy kept pressuring me to be his girlfriend. I told him

several times that I was happy being single and I wasn't looking for a boyfriend. I could tell that

he wasn't happy with that, but we remained friends never the less."

"So why would you say Jeremy's crazy?"

Lisa spoke past her hand as she became teary eyed. "Because one day when I visited

Jeremy at his dorm room, I saw this video clip on his computer while he went to the bathroom. It

was a video of him torturing a rabbit. Oh, Dear God!"

Lisa put both hands over her mouth and began sobbing. "He believes that he killed that

girl that they say he killed. If he would do that to a rabbit, I could see him doing that to a person,

with enjoyment. He was smiling while he was killing that rabbit."

I moved my chair over beside Lisa and wrapped my arm around her. "It's okay, he's behind bars now. He can't come anywhere near you."

Lisa wiped her eyes. "It was nice to go out and eat with you, Greg, but I have to go. I got to talk to Larry and a few other people about Rachel's death."

"Tell me that after all this is over that we'll hang out again. Tell me."

"After all this is over, we'll hang out. Maybe at your place with some friends. I got to go, Greg."

"Peace."

Lisa walked off and I left to drive home.

I turned on the television and found out that the movie Scarface was on again, by flipping through the channels. I watched the film, which starred Al Pacino. There was a scene where Scarface proposes to the boss' girlfriend. What a two faced villain! Scarface's boss gives him a job, protection and a place to stay and this is how Scarface rewards his kindness? I shook my head and glanced over at a newspaper that I bought earlier, now sitting on the floor. There was some brief information about Jeremy's upcoming trial at the top of the page. I turned off the television as the heavy feeling of guilt sunk into my chest. Jeremy had given me an opportunity to change my life and I in exchange betrayed him by going out with his girl. What a friend I was! I was hardly able to carry out the rest of our plans like I told him that I would. I was sissified. I could barely kill Rachel, despite the fact that her boyfriend tried to kill me and even though she represented the type of people that disgusted me. Rachel was a popular snob. People like Rachel looks down on outcasts like me, losers with pointless lives. Looking over all of it, I was glad she was dead. Jeremy had been my boy since high school and never denied me as his friend. The least I could do is carry out the rest of the Washington Bay Vampires' plans for him. I was such a sucker. I let people who could give two shits about me, walk all over me and use me. I was a tool. It was time to stand up for myself. It was time to show love to the people who actually cared for me. It was time to show my love for Jeremy. I'd tell Jeremy about Lisa when the time was right. I grabbed the hunting knife from the suitcase in my closet and began sharpening it in a blade sharpener. As I sharpened the blade, I began to meditate on one of the times back in high school, when I was bullied.

The incident happened during my sophomore year in high school. One day, between classes, I made a trip to the bathroom. As I headed to the urinal, Ryan Jones kicked open the bathroom door and strutted in with his fist balled up. Ryan was over six feet tall and weighed two hundred pounds, all muscle. Ryan approached me, frowning. "Why did you run away from me in the hallway? You heard me calling you. When I call your name, bitch, you better come see what I want. Got it, you dick?"

I nodded with my knees buckling. "Got it, sir."

"Sir…I like that."

Ryan looked down at my new sneakers. "Nice shoes, you mind if I try them on?"

"I can't…my mom says that I can't let anyone try on my shoes."

"You listen to everything that your mother tells you to do. Are you a momma's boy? Come on, let me try them! Just lift up your foot! I'll take them off for you."

"I can't…My mom…"

Ryan cut me off by tackling me to the floor. Putting all his body weight on my legs, he began taking off my shoes. I grunted loudly with watery eyes as I struggled to push Ryan off of me to no avail. Ryan took off my shoes and backhanded me in the nose, causing me to bleed.

Ryan stood up as I laid on the floor in fetal position, holding my nose. Ryan spit on me. "No one tells me no, you stupid bitch."

Ryan picked me up and carried me to a stall where the toilet had stool floating in it. Ryan bent me over the seat, pressing my chest against the front of the toilet. I wiggled and squirmed against the toilet relieve the pressure on my chest and free myself from Ryan grasp, but he was too strong and too strategically focused on keeping me pressed to the toilet. Ryan removed one hand from back and placed his free hand on the back of my head to push my face down in the toilet. I kicked as Ryan pushed my head into the toilet and screamed and choked as he pulled my head out every few seconds.

The sensations came back to me as I remembered. The sounds of the splashing toilet water, the smell of the stool in the toilet, the taste of the toilet water, the sight of the red water caused by my bloody nose, and the feeling of Ryan's palm pressing into my back enraged me as I replayed the incident over and over in my head. Back in the apartment, a mouse ran by my foot into an opening underneath the dishwasher, squeaking and broke my train of thought. I looked downed at the mouse as I sharpened the knife. The mouse ran back from out of the opening and stopped in front of me. I began stomping down on the mouse for several minutes, killing it, as I yelled out, "Ryan, you son of a bitch, you're never going to amount to anything. You're so much of a loser that you have to pick on people smaller than you. I'll kill you. Did you hear me? I'll kill you."

I slid onto the floor with tears running from my eyes. There was mouse blood all over the kitchen and the lower cabinet doors. My boots had streaks all over them and pieces of the mouse were scattered in the center of the room. A chunk with the tail attached was stuck to the bottom of my right boot. I peeled off the sticky red and brown mouse chunk with the knife and spread it

onto the floor. "Sorry, fella, but I needed to let off some steam."

I jumped up, smiling and skipped into my bedroom. I grabbed my Ruger and a half box

of bullets from out of the blue suitcase in my closet and placed them both on the kitchen counter.

I reloaded the clip in the Ruger and placed it in my pocket. I grabbed the suitcase from out my

closet and put the hunting knife in it. I carried the suitcase out to my car drove to Larry's

apartment complex.

#

Eleven

I parked in the lot across from Eric and Jake's building. The sun had gone down before I

arrived at the complex. I waited a few hours in the car, listening to music, looking at how many

times police rode by and through the apartment complex. Every fifteen minutes, the police or so

and flashed a bright light through the driver's side window onto the cars and scenery. I ducked

down into the passenger seat whenever the bright light came near my car. I set my watch for

fifteen minutes and pressed it the next time the cops drove by. Then I hurried out of the car. I

opened my trunk and put the blue suitcase in the passenger's seat. I took out the gown and put it

on over me. I grabbed the fangs and the knife and put them in my pocket under the gown. Last, I

grabbed the mask and put it over my face. According to my watch three minutes had passed. I

looked around from inside my car for people walking in the area. There was no one in sight. I

jogged across the parking lot, staying as low as possible to the ground. I began to walk up the

three flights of stairs to get to room 312.

After going up two flights, I ran into two girls, a red head and a brunette, walking down. I

pulled out the Ruger as they both put up their hands and pled for their lives. The red haired girl

was crying, "Oh my dear God, just let me go, please," repetitively.

The brunette was teary eyed and slowly said, "We'll do whatever you want, just tell us

what to do. Please just let us go. Whatever you say."

I motioned with the gun for both of them to go back up the stairs. "Slowly."

I motion the girls to walk to room 312, to the left of the stairway. "Knock and say you have a flat tire."

I leaned against the wall next to the door on the side farthest from the steps. I looked at my watch. Four more minutes had gone by. The girls knocked and the red head said, "We need to use your phone."

The brunette said, "We have a flat tire" as footsteps could be heard approaching the door.

Eric cracked the door. "You can use my cell phone. Just knock and give it to me when you done."

Eric handed his iPhone to the girls. I snatched the cell phone from his hand and slammed it down, in front of the door. Eric screamed, "You dumb fucker. That's a three hundred dollar phone!"

Eric shut the door and unhooked the chain to unlock it. Eric opened the door and stepped in front of the brunette. "Get away from my fucking door."

Eric glared at the red head and saw me standing next to the door. I aimed the Ruger at him and he put his hands up. I motion him and the girls to go into the room. The red head turned to run down the stairs. I shot her once in the back, dropping her to her knees and sending her tumbling down a flight of stairs. The brunette screamed out loud. "Close your mouth, bitch!" I said, as I shot her in the head.

Eric ran into the apartment. "Jake, get out here! He's got a gun man!"

I walked in and shot Eric once in the back as he ran down the hallway towards a bedroom.

"Dear God," Eric screamed as he fell face first onto the carpet.

Eric curled up into fetal position and began to sob. Then, moaning, he began crawling towards the bedrooms. I walked up behind Eric and fired five more shots into his back. Eric fell onto his chest and his arms began twitching. I looked at the timer on my watch. Just past eleven minutes. The apartment was a three bedroom with a connected kitchen and living room at the front of the apartment. There was a hallway that led to three bedrooms, with the largest one having the door in line with the front door I walked down the hallway with three bedroom doors. I wiggled the knob on the first door to my left and then, finding it locked, kicked it open. I looked into the room. Empty. I moved on to the second. Before I had a chance to wiggle the knob, a shot came through the door and grazed my right shoulder.

"Christ!" I yelled, and put the Ruger in my left hand.

I ran towards the doorway to pick up the brunette. I put the brunette in my right arm and shuffled down the hallway. I leaned her standing up against the door. I stepped back a few feet from the doorway, reloaded the Ruger and fired several shots through the brunette into the room. The bullets showered the walls around the doorway with the brunette's blood. The person in the room fired several shots back. Pieces of the brunette's flesh were ripped off by the hot projectiles and left large gashes between the remaining skin. Some of the girl's ribs protruded through the gashes and the torn openings in her blouse. The gunfire caused her blood to spray throughout the hallway in a mist form. I leaned against the wall next to the doorframe of the second bedroom as the brunette's body made a loud crash onto the floor.

A few moments of silence went by, before I heard footsteps walking towards the door. The doorknob began to slowly turn and then the door was pulled open. Jake stuck his head out, looking down at the brunette on the floor. I shot him in the ear before he even had a chance to notice me along the wall. Clutching his hear, Jake fell on one knee, before collapsing on top of the brunette's back. I looked at the timer on my watch. Sixteen minutes had gone by. Out of time! I flipped Jake over and took the hunting knife out of my pocket. I slit his abdomen open pulled out most of his small intestines. I chopped off a few pieces and tossed them at the door at the end of the hallway.

"Fuck!" I yelled as I heard police sirens approaching.

I pushed Jake off the brunette and flipped her over. I slit open the brunette's stomach and then pulled the fangs from out of my pocket. I slapped her and Jake across the neck with the fangs. I got up, walked out of the apartment and down a flight of stairs. The redhead was knocked out from her fall and there were streaks of blood all over the back of her yellow blouse. I slapped her across the neck with the fangs. The police sirens had gotten very loud. From the stairway window, I could see two police cars driving through the parking lot. I ran back up the stairs and through the third floor hallway towards the stairs on the other end of the building. I stopped at the door of an apartment next to the stairs.

I kneelt/kneeled down under the peephole and knocked on the door. "Police. Are you okay? Open up, I'm a police officer."

I took the Ruger out of my pocket. A tall, white man with black hair opened the door wide open. "What the hell?"

"Get on the ground! Who else is here?"

"It's just me. My roommate is at work."

I step into the apartment and lock the door. "Show me to your room!"

The tall man began walking towards his bedroom at the end of the hallway. I checked the kitchen, the bathroom and his roommate's bedroom, as I followed him towards his room. The tall man's roommate was nowhere to be found. Once I got into his bedroom, I told him to get on his knees. The tall man began to wail, "All I own is yours!"

I took the hunting knife out of my pocket and raised it above the man's head. He collapsed on his chest and cried. I slowly began lowering my blade as the crying of the carried on. The sounds of an ambulance rose through the window. I raised the knife back up. "Jeremy. My brother."

Dropping to one knee, I came down with the knife onto the tall man's back. I stabbed through his heart with one big d stroke, "From the heart. Richard."

I dropped the knife and the man rolled over onto his side, holding his chest. I watched as the muscles in his body spasmed and then became lifeless.

There was a knocking at the front door. I pulled the knife out of the man's back, got up on my feet, slowly shut the bedroom door and locked it. I dragged the man's body and put him in the closet to the left of the door. I turned off the lights in the room and lay down on the bed. The knocking continued on and off for a few minutes before stopping. I lay in the bed for several hours in silence before falling asleep.

#

I woke up to more knocking at the bedroom door. A male voice said, "Brian. You in there, man? I just want to make sure you're okay. There was a murder down the hall. Police are everywhere. They've sectioned off most of the front of the apartment building."

I yawned and pulled the Ruger out of my pocket. I walked to the door and opened it. I aimed the Ruger at the fat black guy standing there. "Keep your fucking mouth close!"

"The ball is in your court."

"Get in the room. Walk in front of the closet."

I took the hunting knife out after the fat guy was facing the closet door. As soon as he started begging for his life, I stabbed him in the neck and then in the back. Oh, boo hoo! The black guy let out a choked yelp as blood blocked the flow of air from his lungs. The body fell to the floor, belly first. I flipped it/him over and sliced open his stomach. I pulled out his intestines and chopped them into five-inch pieces, which I flung across the room. I chopped off his ear and dipped it in the pool of blood forming around the/his body to write the Washington Bay Vampire's trademark message on the wall. I opened the closet and dragged Brian to drop him on top of the fat guy. I split open Brian's stomach and yanked out his intestines. I chopped up Brian's intestines and threw the pieces across the room. I sat on the bed and took off my mask and gown. I went into the bathroom to take a shower. After washing up, I went back into Brian's room to look through his closet. I pulled out a pair of blue jeans that looked about my size and a Ralph Lauren polo shirt to wear. All of Brian's shoes looked too big for me, so I wore his flip flops. I patted Brian and the fat guy down for their wallets, with no success. I went through Brian's dresser and found his wallet in the top drawer. There was eight bucks in his wallet and I put them in my pocket. After I walked into the kitchen to get a trash bag from under the sink, I put the bloody gown, mask, shoes and knife in the bag. I washed my hands and went back into the kitchen to pour me a bowl of Frosted Flakes. I dragged a chair from the kitchen into the bloody room and turned on the television in Brian's room and watch the news coverage on the murders at Jake and Eric's apartment while I ate my cereal.

The news reporter said that the police suspected that the murders were done by the Washington Bay Vampires. No one had been arrested and the police were still looking for leads. A police officer at a televised news conference said that he believed the two women killed at the scene were not the original targets. Instead, they likely caught the vampires in the act of breaking into the apartment and were killed immediately to silence witnesses. The police officer went on to say that he believed that the vampires were not able to leave their full signature because of pressure from police patrol. I turned off the television, grabbed the black garbage bag and walked out the front door. I slung the bag over my shoulder and headed down the stairs next to the apartment.

After I walked down the first flight of stairs, I heard a male voice coming from the third floor. The man said, "Hey. Miami-Dade police. Do you mind giving me a few moments of your time?"

"I got to drop this off in the trash and head to work."

I kept walking down the stairs as the cops said, "Well, if you know anything about what happen last night, please give us a call."

I walked outside of the apartment complex and stood at the bus stop.

The city bus pulled up twenty minutes later and I used two dollars out of Brian's wallet to pay the fare. I rode to a stop a block from my apartment complex. I tapped my pockets and realized that I had left my wallet and keys in my car. I told the maintenance team at my apartment complex that I was locked out. A maintenance worker opened my door for me.

#

I stayed in my apartment for the next three days until I got a notice in the mail that my car had been towed. I called my mom and told her that I needed two hundred and twenty dollars to get my car back. I took the bus to my Mom's house to get the money and took the bus again to the towing company to pick up my car.

I laid low for a few days to catch up on my homework and get a little more sleep between school, work and a nightlife filled with murder.

#

Later that week, while I was studying for chemistry, I dozed off and began thinking. The two girls I killed near Eric and Jake's apartment might work against my insanity plea. A lot of the evidence seemed to say that I strategically pressured the girls to head to Eric's room. Their D. N. A. was on the door from knocking and the brunette's D. N. A. was against Jake's bedroom door. In addition to this, neither Eric nor the red head had their stomachs sliced open, meaning that the killer was aware that the police were nearby. I'm not a psychologist, but the evidence made the killer sound more like someone led by their intelligence than their insanity. The prosecutor might look at these facts and say that the murders of Eric, Jake and the two girls were premeditated. I closed my chemistry book and began watching the news on television.

The news was covering an update on Jeremy's upcoming trial. The female news reporter said that the case had been pushed back because a few of the key witnesses were deceased. The news reporter went on to say that the district attorney, the police and the families of the victims feared that Jeremy might walk out of the trial a free man. I turned off the television and walked outside to my car. I drove to Vulture prison.

I signed in to see Jeremy and sat at a visitor's booth. Jeremy came to his chair with a grin across his face. I smiled. "I see you're feeling better. I heard about the delay in your trial, they said that you might walk."

"I feel great. Apparently, some of the witnesses were murdered. Like you said, no witnesses, no murder."

"That's what it is! Turns out the two witnesses, Eric and Jake that claimed to see you at the party that night suddenly…." I point at myself as I say, "Were taken out."

Jeremy frowned. "I told you, Greg, I didn't want you to jeopardize our plans for anything foolish. I can take care of myself. My mom got me a good lawyer. I could have possibly beaten the case even if the two were alive."

A stoic look comes over my face. "I did this for us. For you. I don't like seeing you behind bars, Jeremy. You're my brother, man. We are supposed to start a new life somewhere on an exotic island. How can I start a new life without my partner in crime?"

Jeremy sternly said, "I appreciate what you've done. With the case weakened because of lack of witnesses, my lawyer should be able to set me free easily. But, what I want more than being set free is to finish carrying out our plans. So, I need you to leave all my troubles alone and take care of business. If you keep it up, and they are able to make a connection between what you are doing and my situation, it's going to hurt our plea when we go public about everything."

"Alright, I'll leave it alone. Glad you're feeling better and that things are working out for you. But there is one more thing. I really hate to ruin your mood, but I think it's time I told you. I've become friends with Lisa. Lisa Jones."

"Friends. In what way? You guys study together?"

"We've done some shopping together. And we've went out to eat once."

Jeremy crossed his arms. "Wow! So you and Lisa. Well, she wasn't my girlfriend. I was just a friend to her and I'm friends with you. I mean, people should want to see their friends happy, right? I'm happy for you, man. I did say that you can have her, right?"

Jeremy's eyes were watery. I put my hands in my lap. "If you don't want me to date her, just say so. It's my brother before a girl. You were with me before I met Lisa. I wasn't trying to hurt you, man. I just happen to meet her, while I was out taking care of our plans and one thing happened after another. I wouldn't have even pursued her out of respect for you, but the way you talked about her... It seemed that you were over her. Sorry, bro."

"No need to apologize. I'll find someone else. Where there is one girl there's another. I've been done with her for a while, anyway."

"Great. I'm glad that you're okay about Lisa and me going out."

"I got to go, Greg. It's close to lunch time and I don't want to miss out on the dessert for the day."

"Take care."

I left the prison feeling refreshed. Jeremy didn't mind that I was seeing Lisa and there was a very good chance he would walk. Larry was the only witness left who had seen Jeremy at the party. The case would probably lean on Larry's eye witness testimony that Jeremy killed Sarah.

#

Later that night, as I was watching a television show on how the Chicago police department had solved a murder that had happen fifteen years ago, a chill ran up my spine. The murder case was given to a new detective. On a hunch, the detective decided to reinterview the witnesses and one came forward with some new information on the case. Based on the new information and the signed statement from the witness, the police were able to charge a previous suspect with the murder. The suspect was convicted of capital murder based on the testimony of one witness and circumstantial evidence.

Jeremy and I were foolish for believing that Jeremy's case would be a cool breeze. I walked into my closet and pulled out the black garbage bag with all the evidence in it. I took the bloody gown, shoes, gloves, and mask out of the g bag. I washed the m and put them in a new black garbage bag. I washed the bloody fangs and hunting knife in my kitchen sink. I reloaded the clip in my Ruger and placed the Ruger in my pocket, along with the knife and fangs. I carried the garbage bag with my vampire outfit in it to my car.

I drove to Larry's apartment complex and drove through the parking lot to the exit on the other side, examining the area. There was a cop car posted at every apartment building. The police were not playing any games.

I drove back home and saw a cop car at almost every light within a mile of Larry's apartment complex. I sat down at my dining room table and sent a text to Lisa. *Let's get something to eat tonight.*

I waited ten minutes and got no reply. I opened my chemistry book and then heard my phone chirp. I had received a text message from Lisa that said, I'm *going out to eat with a couple of friends at the Applebee's on Washington Street, come join us in thirty minutes.*

I put on a blue and white striped, long sleeve shirt by Ralph Lauren. I bought the shirt online, the week before, as my reward for spending time to research on how to better my craft. I had done several Google searches on how to kill someone without a guilty conscience. I read through several results that popped up, of which were mostly Christian sites. The Christian sites and several people within various forums stated similar things relating to what a conscience is, why we have a conscience, why a conscience is important and how to deal with guilt. Most Christian sites said to pray and ask the Lord for forgiveness to free yourself of guilt. Some bloggers stated that your conscience is innate and gives you a sense of morality; to eliminate your conscience would be a tragedy, as you would lose touch with humanity, lose your ability to love and become nothing but a robotic being. Another blogger, named Deviant2433, gave some helpful information. He wrote that all you have to do is think of all the people that would make you feel guilty about any supposedly wrong act and questioned their motives for making you feel guilty. Is it because they truly want to see you do better or do they want you to feel guilty out of spite for you. If you constantly assume that your accusers are charging you wrong doing out of spite, it will make their accusations seem unrespectable. I wrote down Deviant2433's input on the subject. In addition to the anger displacement method that Jeremy taught me to hype myself up to kill people, I would use Deviant2433's free conscience theory to aide me in my murder spree.

I drove to Applebee's with a smile on my face. Lisa had invited me out to eat and drink with her friends. The fun that Lisa would have with her friends would distract her from how much alcohol that she was drinking. If Lisa was drunk enough, she might go home with me tonight. I drove to Applebee's and walked around the dining area, searching for Lisa. Lisa was nowhere in sight. I walked outside sent a text to Lisa. *Change of plans?*

My friends canceled on me, but we can still hang out. Meet me at Melrose Park on Broad Street, near the sailor statue.

Glad that you didn't stand me up. I'm on my way.

I drove to the park and parked my car at a meter. I put eight quarters in the meter to give me two hours. Melrose Park had lots of trees, walkways, benches and statues around three large ponds. The park was about two miles in diameter. I had been there several times with my mother to walk the dog when I was younger. Melrose Park sat between campus and my old home. The sailor statue sat near the center of the park. Out of all the statues that Lisa and I could have met by, Lisa chose the one about a mile from where I had parked. I walked towards the statue, singing my favorite rap song by Eminem, "Same Song and Dance". The song is about a serial killer going through his daily life of kidnapping his victims and killing them. The methods that the serial killer used had all become routine. Every crime had become the same song and dance. I made it to the sailor statue and began walking around it to look for Lisa to no success. I stopped

searching and leaned against the statue, clinching my fist. "The stupid broad has stood me up."

Suddenly, I heard a familiar male voice approaching, a voice that gave me Goosebumps.

"Hello Greg."

Larry stepped into light under a light post, aiming a pistol at me. My teeth chattered.

"Larry, long time no see. Where's Lisa?"

"She's not coming. She was busy with her school work."

"I just sent her a text and she responded. Why wouldn't she let me know that she wasn't

coming?"

Larry held up Lisa's phone with his other hand. "I took her phone. I met up with her

earlier today. We were supposed to go to Applebee's and meet up with you. I convinced them to

go to another restaurant. I stole her phone while she was in the bathroom and left before she was

able to text you and tell you about the change in plans. She's probably eating dinner with her

friends, right now as we speak."

"You're not going to kill me, Larry. You have no reason to. I haven't talk to the police,

and why would you want to put yourself in hot water with the police again after knowing that

they want to pin a case you?"

"Better I get you before you get me. Who else would have killed Jake and Eric? And

Rachel, for that matter. Who else would have a motive? I killed your best friend, so you wanted

to kill my best friends. With your last and only friend in jail and with me being the only witness,

it only makes since that the Washington Bay Vampires would kill me next. Oh, come on, Greg.

You don't think that I know by now who the Washington Bay Vampires are? Better yet, *were*. I

figured it out after you killed Rachel and then Jake and Eric, back to back. Those killings in that order had to be more than random. I could've revealed your identity to the police, but I had rather taken care of you myself for murdering those close to me. The way you killed those people, you disgustingly sick monsters. There are so many people that would love to find out who you guys are and talk to you about the murders. Unfortunately, they are never going to get that chance. You guys were a hot topic on campus. And now the Vampires will be a hot lead for the police to look into about your murder."

Each statue in the park was encircled by a field of grass. The grass around the sailor statue was worn down and there was lots of small pebbles scattered throughout the dirt. As Larry pulled back the hammer on his pistol, I kicked some of the rocks towards his face and took off running behind the statue. Larry jumped back and fired a round towards me. The bullet ricocheted off the statue and the shot echoed. I ran onto the sidewalk as Larry chased me, firing rounds continuously. I zig zagged towards the exit, a mile away. I was sprinting at full speed and my eyes were locked on the long path ahead of me. I was sweating all over and my legs were becoming heavy after running about a quarter of a mile. Whenever I tried to slow down to catch my breath and look back to see if Larry was still behind me, I would hear a gunshot ricochet. I had about a fifty meter lead on Larry. I saw a statue in the near distance. The statue was a copper model of three men signing a document at a table. The platform for the model stood about five feet high. I ran behind it pulled myself onto the ledge behind one of the men. I pulled my Ruger out as I leaned my back against the copper legs. Larry ran behind and a few feet past the statue before stopping to survey the area. I fired four shots at Larry and hit him twice in the back. Larry fell to his knees and then on his face, twitching. I jumped down and walked over to his body. I knelt down and put the Ruger to the back of Larry's head. "Tell Richard that I said hi, after you apologize to him."

I fired three rounds into Larry's skull. Then I took off running back to my car. I got in and drove home.

I tossed my sweaty clothes into the washing machine and jumped in the shower. After showering, I went to the television in my living room. I began watching a show on cold case files that were recently solved. In one cold case file, the detective had reexamined the evidence and spoke to a suspect that the police had overlooked. After questioning the suspect and getting probable cause, the police were able to get a warrant to search the man's house for a pistol. Sweat broke out on my forehead as I saw forensics match the bullets from the murder with the man's pistol. I quickly turned off the television and grabbed my Ruger, along with the bullets and clips that I had purchased with it. I stashed the Ruger and accessories in an old duffle bag. I put the duffle bag in my trunk and drove to a park nearby that had a pond.

I walked along the pond and picked up a large white stone, weighing about thirty pounds. I took the duffle bag out of trunk and put the stone in it. I zipped up the bag and put it in the passenger side seat. As I drove home, I stopped on the side of a long bridge, sitting above a river. It was around three o'clock in the morning and there were few cars driving by. I grabbed the duffle bag and got out of my car. I threw the duffle bag into the river. I drove home, washed the sweat from face and fell asleep in my bed.

#

Twelve

I woke up to knocking at my door. I opened the door in my pajamas. A dark haired, muscular detective, wearing glasses flashed his badge. "My name is Detective Ronald Nelson. I'm investigating a murder and I was wondering if you could come down to the station to talk with me."

"Sure. I don't see any reason why not."

"Do you mind if I have a few officers search your residence while you're down at the station with me?"

"That's fine. Whatever I can do to help you solve you case. Really? Someone was murdered. Around here? In this apartment complex?"

"At another apartment complex, about a mile away."

I got into the police car and was driven to the police station. I was lead into an interview room and given a cup of coffee.

After a few minutes, Detective Nelson entered the room. Ronald said, "We are investigating five murders that all took place at the Blue Springs apartment complex. You are not under arrest, but we would like to ask you a few questions. What is your full name?"

"Gregory Rotten."

"Greg. Do you own a firearm?"

"Yes. Well, I did own one. But someone broke into my apartment, a while back and stole my gun, along with a few other things."

"Did you report the burglary?"

"No offense, sir. But when I was younger, my mother reported a burglary. My PlayStation was stolen. I am still out of a PlayStation and the case is still unsolved. I never hear about many burglaries being solved. What's the point?"

"Burglaries are some of the hardest cases to solve, but some still are. You should have reported the burglary. Someone may have seen the suspects and been able to identify them. What kind of gun did you own?"

"A Ruger."

"Do you own any hunting knives?"

"No. I don't have a reason to own one."

"Do you know of any one that may have wanted to break into your home?"

"No one. I don't have any enemies and I don't have much that would cause someone to be envious of me."

"Tell me about your friends."

"I don't any friends at the moment. I recently lost two. One is locked up and the other was killed by the Washington Bay Vampires. He was in the newspaper. I saw him die in front of me, right before the vampires tried to kill me."

"That's terrible. What are your friends' full names?"

"Richard Walters and Jeremy Winters."

"Oh, yeah! I know about Jeremy Winters, but I don't remember hearing anything about a guy named Richard Walters. Another detective must be working on that case. Don't worry! We're going to catch whoever killed your friend and make sure he is locked up for a long time. I'm very sorry to hear about your friends, but I need to ask you about a few people that you may know. Do you know or have you ever heard of Eric Beard, Jake Smalls, Tiffany Andrews, Karen Smith, Roger Ross or Larry Berg?"

"I know of Larry, Jake and Eric. I met them briefly at a triple Alpha frat party."

"Did you get into any conflict with Larry, Jake or Eric during this party?"

"No. Not all."

"The reason that I'm asking you all this is because Eric, Jake, and Larry are dead. Bullet fragments from the gun you had purchased from Joe's Gun Shop were recovered. You say that the gun was stolen. So if the officer at your apartment can verify that you no longer own the gun, then you have nothing to be worried about. Do you know of anyone that might want Larry, Eric or Jake dead?"

"They all seemed like fun guys to party with. I can't fathom why someone would want them dead."

"Would you be willing to submit your DNA, so that we could potentially eliminate you as a suspect in the murders?"

"I'd rather not."

"Why is that?"

"I don't know anything about those murders, so there is no reason for me to give you my DNA."

"Would you be willing to take a polygraph?"

"Am I free to go?"

"You are here voluntarily."

"Thank you, detective."

The detective walked me out of the room and escorted me to a police officer waiting with a car outside of the station. Detective Ronald gave me his card, "If you have information on the murders or if you decide to come by and submit your D. NA., give me a call."

I got into the car and was driven back to my apartment.

I turned on my television and began watching the local news. One of the stories covered was the murder of Larry Berg. The reporter said that the police suspected that the Washington Bay Vampires were responsible because the gun used in the killing match the gun used to kill Eric, Jake, the redheaded girl, named Tiffany Andrews, and the brunette named Karen Smith. The reporter said that police struggled to give motives for the deaths. Their confusion was due to the fact that the victims were killed in a manner that did not fit a typical murder by the Washington Bay Vampires.

#

A few days later, I woke up and went into my living room to watch the news on television. I bit my nails as I viewed the stories. Thanksgiving break had begun and I finished all my schools work over the weekend. One of the stories covered was the release of Jeremy Winters. I smiled when the reporter said that the state would release Jeremy on November 25, Thanksgiving Day, because of lack of evidence. I turned off the television, got dressed and drove to Vulture prison.

I signed in to talk to Jeremy and sat at a conference booth. He sat down at the conference booth. "How are things with Lisa?"

"Pretty good, I guess. I was supposed to go out for drinks with her this past Wednesday, but I cancelled on her. I had to take care of some personal business."

"Well at least she knows what it's like now to be stood up. I'm glad that things are working out between you guys."

"Maybe once you get out I'll see if she has a friend and maybe we can double date. I know being locked up a while has got you e thirsty for some female attention."

"I'd like that."

"How does it feel to be getting out, man? Now we can hang out again. I'm so excited. It'll be like old times and maybe now that you name is cleared, you can talk with your pops again."   "Maybe."

"What's wrong? You don't seem that enthusiastic about leaving. Don't you hate being locked up here?"

Jeremy slouched and supported his head with his palm, "Of course. I'm just a little agitated that you didn't listen to me. But now that I'm free. I guess I'll get it over. I know that you were just looking out me. I can't be mad at you for being a good friend."

"No, you can't. When you get out, you can stay at my place and have Thanksgiving with my family. That is, if you aren't spending Thanksgiving with your family"

"Thanks. I'll crash at your place, but I talked with my mom today and she really wanted me to spend Thanksgiving with her and my dad."

"So you and your Dad are okay again?"

"Something like that. It doesn't matter to him if I did it or not, it's just the fact that I was even accused of something like this that bothers him."

"Do you think that he thinks that you killed Sarah?"

"Yes. The first time that I talked to him after being arrested, my father told me that he knew it was only a matter of time before I got caught up in some mess and was kicked out of school. He always felt that raising me was a burden because of all the trouble I had gotten into during elementary and high school."

"Maybe, he'll change his thinking about you now that you're a free and innocent man/"

"Maybe. Until he finds out about…our plans."

"Well, maybe a few years after our plan, he'll come back around to the fact that you're his son and that he loves you very much."

Jeremy nodded. "I hope so."

"I got to head to work in about an hour, so I'm going to head out. Give me a call, when they release you and I'll pick you up."

"See you Thursday."

#

Loud knocking at my door woke me up from my sleep. I looked at the clock and it was about nine' o clock in the morning, Thanksgiving Day. I walked to the door in my pajamas. "What's up? What do you need?"

"Wake up, bro, it's Jeremy."

I opened the door and gave Jeremy a hug and some dap. "Jeremy. How did you get here? I told you that you could call me and I would pick you up. How does it feel to be a free man?"

"Freaking awesome. I told my mom that you would pick me up, but she earnestly wanted to see me. So she sent my cousin to pick me up and take me home."

"So the first thing you did after coming home was leave your stuff at your parents and then come to my place?"

"What's wrong with that? You told me I could crash here."

"Nothing is wrong with that. I just thought that you would want to spend a little time with your parents first."

"I tried to. I spoke with my mother and lots of my family members for thirty minutes or so until my dad woke up from all the commotion. But he refused to acknowledge my presence and when I confronted him about it, he flipped out and told me to leave his home. My mom said that maybe I could come back later after my dad had calmed down a bit."

"All of that happened this morning?"

"Yes. About a half hour before I came here. I told my mom that I could stay at your place until my dad calmed down and I had my cousin drop me off here."

"How did you know where I stayed at?"

"I passed by your mom's place and she gave me your address"

"Well, make yourself at home. I got some lunch meat in the fridge to make sandwiches and a couple of boxes of cereal in the cabinet. Eat anything that you like."

I showed Jeremy around my apartment and pointed at my couch. "You can sleep on the couch. I have some extra comforters in my bedroom closet. I'm going to jump back in the bed for a few hours. You can turn on the television and watch whatever. I have an extra bar of soap and some towels in the bathroom closet, if you want to take a shower."

"Cool. I'll wake you if I decide to go back to my parents' house."

I handed Jeremy the remote control and went to bed.

Exhausted, I slept until the sun was setting. I walked out of into the living room. "Jeremy get up, it's six in the afternoon."

Jeremy was nowhere to be found. I guessed that Jeremy decided to head back to his parent's place, so I drove to my parents' place for Thanksgiving dinner.

After eating and spending a few hours with my folks, I drove home with a stuffed stomach.

I lay down on the couch to watch the news. The news was covering the murder of Larry Berg. The reporter said that the police had no leads but suspected the perpetrator is someone that Larry knew. The police issued a ten thousand dollar reward for any information leading to the arrest of the murderer. I turned down the volume on my television as I heard a loud banging at the door.

I yelled, "Jeremy, I thought that you were going to wake me up when you left."

A few moments went by and there was no answer at the door. I walked into my kitchen and pulled a steak knife out of my dishwasher. My knees were buckling as I whispered, "Larry?"

There was near silence in the room for five minutes. I walked to the door with a knife in hand and opened the door a crack. "Larry?"

I didn't see anyone outside or near my door. I shut the door and sat down. There was a few knocks at the window near my couch. It sounded like someone was throwing pebbles at the window. I peeked through the blinds but I didn't see anyone. I sat down on the couch and turned the volume back up on the television. There was a loud bang at the door and then some more knocking at the window. I put my shoes on, gripped the steak knife tightly and opened the front door. I walked outside and around my apartment, scanning the area to no success. I sighed and walked into my apartment.

I looked down at the carpet and screamed. "Jesus Christ!"

There were streaks of blood all over the carpet. A cat's head was on the floor, separated from the body which lay nearby. The cat's limbs were torn from its torso and scattered throughout the room. I heard the door shut behind me and before I could turn around, someone had pulled my head back into a choke hold. I stabbed the person behind me in the forearm and they screamed, "Greg! It's me. Jeremy."

I dropped the knife and Jeremy let me go. "Dang it. You cut me, man. I was just joking with you."

"You shouldn't have snuck up behind me. And what were you thinking with bringing a dead cat in here. My nerves are as bad as they can get. The police just searched my apartment for trace evidence and Larry just tried to kill me."

"I'm sorry, man. I didn't know you were so stressed. I just haven't seen my boy in a while and I had to catch up on old times."

I said aloud, "You know, it's funny that I can run my fingers through someone's intestines..... and gaze upon the sight of a person's exposed organs without feeling nauseated, but the sight of that dead cat makes me feel sick."

I crossed my arms, "Where did you get it from? Get it out of here, man."

"Alright, I will. You got some bandages that I can put over this cut?"

The steak knife that I had bought from the dollar store was pretty dull. The knife had only penetrated Jeremy's first layer of skin. I went into my bathroom and pulled out a box with some gauze and large bandages. Jeremy rinsed his cut in the sink with hydrogen peroxide. Jeremy put some gauze and then a large bandage over the cut. "I know to never sneak up on you again."

"Stop acting like a baby. You weren't cut that deep."

"Imagine if I had tried to tackle you. You probably would have stabbed me in the neck. Got any plastic bags or newspaper?"

"I got some plastic bags under the sink. You can use the dish rag to clean up the blood. I have some bleach on the shelf above the dryer. Make sure you throw it away after you clean that mess up."

I sat down on the couch and began watching *the Simpsons* as Jeremy cleaned the blood off the floor. As Jeremy tied up the cat's head in a plastic grocery bag, I said, "You know, you were right about killing. I got upset a while back and wound up killing a mouse in my anger. I thought I would feel ashamed about it, but it turned out to be the best stress relief that I had ever exploited."

"It is a soothing tool. Whenever I get frustrated with someone or the way things are going. I seem to feel better after I find something or someone to displace my anger onto, whether it's a wall to punch a hole in, or a dog to throw down some stairs or a cat to chop up. I seem to feel much better afterwards. Inmates aren't allowed to have pets in jail. The best stress relief in there was cutting up my arms with a spoon that I sanded down and sharpened against concrete."

"You were stressed about not being able to talk with your father."

"That, and the fact that I couldn't be out there with you terrorizing people. At night in prison, I would think about how good it felt to stab Melvin and that girl over and over again. When I stabbed them, I felt a warm, tingling sensation in my body. At that moment, I was so concentrated on killing them that my mind was free of all my troubles and worries. It felt good to know that by taking a life, I could make people suffer in a way that was out of their control in the same way that we suffered on campus."

"You killed the cat because your dad made you upset today?"

"No, I killed the cat out of frustration because I was in the mood to go out and kill someone with you, but I felt that you wouldn't want take care of our plans on Thanksgiving. I caught that cat roaming in my parent's backyard and killed it in the garage while they were watching a movie with my aunts, uncles, and cousins."

I nodded and leaned back against the couch. Jeremy smiled. "Let's take someone out tonight. Let's make it part of my welcome home party."

"On Thanksgiving? Come on. No. Who would you want to get? We'd have to plan. Next on our list is a professor. We'd have to follow one and find out where they live. Maybe some time next week when school starts back up."

"Not necessarily. I can get a professor's number from the student phone book and trace their address to the number."

"You wouldn't know if a professor had his or her family over or what kind of police surveillance is in the area they live in."

"It should take no longer than an hour or so to scope out the area. Hopefully, if we can find a professor that is not out visiting relatives and if that professor is at home alone, then we'll take him or her out, but if there is someone with him or her, we'll wait till next week."

"For all we know there could be police watching us outside as we speak. You just got released from jail for a crime that the police believe you did, and the police suspect that I killed Jake and Eric. I'm sure that they'll keep a close eye on us."

"Eventually, we have to get back out there and finish our plans. We can't wait too long or else the hype surrounding our murders will fade. And eventually we want them to catch us in the act, right? There is only one other person that we need to take care of besides a professor, and if we get caught before we get to him, I still think that we'll have enough hype to get a good book deal."

"Richard would have wanted us to finish our plans completely."

Jeremy placed the dish rag down. I turned off the television. "Don't ruin everything that we have put together."

"That's what I had told you and you didn't listen, did you?"

"Alright. Let's get some supplies first. You need a mask, a knife and a gown. When we get back, we pick a professor and look him or her up online. But next time, let's take a little bit more time to plan a murder."

Jeremy smiled and nodded. I put my shoes on and grabbed my light jacket from the closet. Jeremy and I drove to Wal-Mart and bought a pair of black stockings, two hunting knives, a couple two-pronged meat forks and a black sheet.

Back at the apartment, I turned on my laptop and Jeremy went to the Washington Bay University homepage. Jeremy clicked on the staff directory and began looking at all the names listed. I tapped Jeremy on the shoulder. "I'll start putting together your outfit."

I walked into the dining room with the shopping bags and pulled out the gown and stockings. I cut the end of one stocking leg off and set it aside. I laid the black sheet across the table and cut a head hole in the center of the sheet with a pair of scissors from the kitchen. I cut a two foot by four foot strip off the long ends of the twin size sheet. I folded the sheet up and place the home made mask on top. Jeremy said, "Greg. I need your credit card."

"For what? I'm not paying for porn."

"Take it in the face, Greg. I need your credit card to find out where Professor Thomas James lives. I found a site that can trace his address by phone number. They won't give me the address until I pay them."

"How much?"

"Thirty dollars. I'll give it back to you when I get back in school and on my feet. Take one for the team."

I shook my head and pulled my wallet out of my pocket. I gave Jeremy my card and he bought Professor James' address information online. I sat down on the couch next to Jeremy. "Why Professor James? Who is he, anyway?"

"He's my precalculus teacher. He's a jerk off."

"No personal killings. Remember Sarah? We don't want to have to go through that again."

"Yeah, but this is different, I don't know Mr. James personally. He's no more than an acquaintance, and besides, you did just pay thirty dollars to get his address. Would you like me to pay another thirty bucks to find another professor?"

"I just don't understand why you couldn't choose someone that neither of us knows."

"Like who? And what could anyone else do for our name? I thought about it and there really is no professor that stands out above the others. Some have worked at the university longer than others and some are on committees at the school, but there are very few professors that everyone on campus has come in contact with. Really doesn't matter what professor we kill, it'll have the same effect on our name. My hatred for him will make it easier to for me take him out. Jail has made me a little emotionally rusty on the murder scene. I need something to put me back in the right mentality. You've had plenty of practice since I've been gone. I helped you at one time through the process. Now you can help me through the process."

"Seeing that the death of the professor won't do much for us, how can we use this killing to add more fuel to our fire?"

"Remember that the more shocking part about our murders is not that we killed someone, but how we killed them. We'll cut Professor James into several pieces and leave words with each body part that will make our signature message when combined."

I nodded. "Well, let's head out then."

I handed Jeremy a meat fork, a hunting knife and the outfit that I had made for him. I wrote down Mr. James' address and walked to the car with Jeremy. Jeremy said, "Can I see your tire iron?"

I nodded and popped the trunk as I got into the driver's seat. Jeremy hopped into the passenger seat carrying the tire iron. We drove towards Professor James' house. We stopped and parked near a stop sign a block away. The professor lived on a long strip of a land within a suburban neighborhood, near a park centered in the middle. A stream flowed behind the park and all the houses on the long strip of land, separated from them by twenty feet of grass. . I tapped Jeremy on the shoulder. "We'll drive slowly by to see if anyone is inside and then, a block ahead, I'll get out and walk around to see what activity is going on in or near the house."

We drove past the house and saw all the lights were on. A group of people gathered in the living room, visible through the windows. I stopped the car and Jeremy sternly said, "Drive back in front of the house and wait for me."

"What do you plan to do? His whole family is there."

"Drive in front of his house."

#

Thirteen

I put the car in reverse and backed up to the professor's house. Jeremy slapped my shoulder. "Keep the car running and pop the trunk."

I popped the trunk as Jeremy got out with the tire iron. Jeremy hid the tire iron behind his back. Jeremy walked up and rang the doorbell. A lady answered and Jeremy said something to her with a smile. The lady nodded and shut the door. Jeremy looked back at me, still smiling. A frowning bald man opened the door and Jeremy smiled back at him. The man was about six feet tall with a beer gut and glasses. Jeremy walked down two steps on the stairs leading to the door. Jeremy motioned the man to come outside as he said something to the man which I couldn't make out. The man walked out the door and closed it behind him. Jeremy walk back up on the patio a foot or two from the man. The man began poking Jeremy in the chest as he sneered, "How dare you come on my property with this garbage. Why didn't you call me if you needed to talk? I don't change grades for anyone. I don't care if my whole class is failing. I'll give every one of them a failing grade and you are no exception. Don't you ever show your face here again! Excuse me. I'm watching a movie."

Jeremy was frowning and balled his fist up. The professor turned around to walk back in the door and Jeremy wacked the professor with the tire iron across the head. Jeremy smacked the professor several times across the head as Professor James lay passed out across the ground. Jeremy began to drag the professor by his legs down the stairs and towards my car. I got out. "Jeremy, what are you doing? Out in the open. No mask. Are you crazy?"

"Help me put him in the trunk."

As I stooped down to help Jeremy pick up the professor, two older men came running out of the front door towards us with butcher knives. The older of the two men, with long hair trailing behind him as he ran, screamed, "You sorry little maggots drop him now!"

Jeremy and I quickly threw the professor in the trunk and ran along the driver's side to hop back into the car. I locked the doors as Jeremy shut his. The man with the long hair broke one the back window on the passenger's side with his knife. Jeremy picked up my suitcase as a shield. I sped off as both men began to reach and stab at Jeremy through the broken window. The men were pressed against the car as they reached through the window. The two guys rolled off the car and fell onto the floor as the car sped by and rubbed against their legs. I yelled, "What were you thinking? Now they know what we looked like. They have a description of us and everything!"

"They don't know who we are, though."

"But they can pick us out of a lineup!"

"More than likely they are just visiting for the weekend. They each have jobs and won't have time to sit around for the police to get a line up. By the time we are caught, they probably won't even remember what we look like."

"You told that lady your name."

"I gave her a false name. I told him that Jacob Lenard needed to speak with him about his grade in his class. We're eventually going to turn ourselves in anyway, right? So the families of the victims are going to find out what we look like anyway." "Then why did we need a mask and outfit?"

"We need them for our theme."

"Okay. You know. So why kill him out in the open with no mask? How does that help our theme or let the police know that the murder was done by the Washington Bay Vampires? Not to mention, this is a personal murder. Something like premeditated first degree murder because when the cops check my laptop, they are going to see that you looked up his address. This is going to ruin our insanity plea."

"You have a point. Pull over."

I pulled the car over. "Yes?"

"Let me drive. I have a plan."

I crawled over into the passenger's seat and Jeremy got into the driver's seat. Jeremy drove back in the direction of the professor's house. I yelled, "Jeremy, they probably called the cops by now! You're going to get us arrested."

"It takes about five to ten minutes for the cops to respond. All I need is two."

Jeremy turned with the front end of the car facing the house so that the car was blocking the street. Through a window on the right side of the house, we saw a group of people at a table talking. Jeremy backed up the car a few feet, got out and grabbed the tire iron from the back seat. Jeremy charged towards the house and threw the tire iron through the dining room window. He ran back to the car as the man with the long hair and the man with the short curls came running out. Jeremy hopped in and pressed hard on the gas as the men ran in front of the car. As Jeremy sped ahead, he hit the man with the long hair. He rolled onto the windshield, cracking it, and rolled over the car onto the street. Jeremy continued speeding a few more feet and ran over the man with the short curls. He got caught up in the wheel and axle, causing the car to swerve. Jeremy let go of the accelerator and pressed on the brake to stop the swerving. Jeremy put the car in park as we heard police sirens in the far distance. Jeremy screamed, "Give me your mask! I'm going to get the lady that saw me. I want you to drive home as soon as I get out of the car. I'll swim across the stream after I kill the lady and hide out in the woods until the cops leave."

"No good. The cops will send out the dogs to find you. They'll trace your scent and find you across the stream."

"Good thinking. Okay, meet me on the other side of the woods, across the stream. This street circles around through a few busy intersections to the park, and then goes across the stream and through the forest. It should take me no longer than twenty minutes to get there."

"Hurry, Jeremy. I'll see you soon."

Jeremy shut the door and I backed up the car to untangle the man with short curls from the front wheel on the passenger side. A human arm flung out under the wheel of the car when I backed up. The man with the curls laid on his stomach with blood geysering from, where his arm used to be. The man's head had been snapped back across his shoulder blades with a ripped opening across his neck that exposed his larynx. I drove off down the street, heading for the other side of the woods.

After a mile or so, I saw cop cars going in the opposite direction at the intersection of a busy street. I drove around to the park. The park was located on a strip of land that outlined the stream across from residential homes, and was secluded from the merging busy streets. The park contained a playground and a bike path. I parked in the lot next to a baseball field that sat next to the park and a black top parking lot next to the baseball field. I got out of the car and took off my white T-shirt and wiped the blood off my windshield and front hood with it. I threw the bloody shirt in my car and walked over to the park. I sat on a bench and took several deep breaths to cause the trembling in my arms and legs to cease. Thirty minutes or so went by and then Jeremy came running out of the forest. Jeremy jogged over to me, sweating profusely, bleeding and breathing deeply. Jeremy knelt down in front of me. "We have to get out of here. I'm sure the cops are on my trail. I killed the lady that saw me."

"Jeremy, your arm is bleeding. What happened?"

"The lady and her daughter or niece pulled knives on me as soon as I entered the house. She and the girl both stabbed me as we wrestled for control.."

"We need to get you to a hospital."

"The cuts aren't that bad. Her daughter had a tiny pocket knife and the lady didn't hit an artery. We can stitch up the cut at your place. Where's the car? I barely made it out the back door before I heard the police pull up in front of the house. They might be on their way over here now."

We sprinted to my car and stopped at Wal-Mart to buy some rubbing alcohol, gauze, tape, stitches and pins. We began driving home when we heard a loud thumping sound coming from the back seat. I looked in my rear view mirror to see if something had bumped into my car, to no avail. I drove to the forested area near my house and parked in the visitor's parking. The thumping had gotten louder and I could hear Professor James yelling, "I can't breathe in here. Someone please open the trunk."

I opened the suitcase in the back seat and pulled out a hunting knife. Jeremy grabbed my hand as I opened the driver's side door. "Let me do the honor."

I wrapped Jeremy's arm with gauze and taped it down tightly. I handed Jeremy the cars keys and hunting knife and Jeremy got out of the car. I looked at Jeremy in the rear view mirror as he popped the trunk. Through the gap between the door and the trunk, I could see Jeremy's stomach and part of the knife. Professor James shouted, "I'll change your grade. Please stop!"

The knife disappeared from view and then I heard Professor James shriek loudly. Jeremy began stabbing Professor James rapidly, over and over again. I could see the blade appearing and disappearing through the crack in the trunk. Professor James shrieked each time. With each stoke that Jeremy made with the knife, the volume of Professor James' cries got lower. After the cries

of the professor died out, Jeremy shut the trunk and hopped back into the passenger seat. He had

streaks of blood all over his face and blue T-shirt and his gauze was bloody all over, especially

where his cut had reopened. Jeremy held his forehead. "Man, I feel kind of dizzy."

"You're still bleeding. Maybe we need to get you to the hospital."

"I should be okay until we get back home to your place. Let's get rid of the body first."

"Let me see the cut on your back. You sure it was a small blade? You look a little pale."

"I should be alright. The hospital will probably be the first place the cops look after

seeing all the blood in the house."

"You said the cuts weren't that deep. If you bleed all over, then that means that you were

cut pretty deep. Better the police pick you up at the hospital than pick you off the ground

somewhere, dead. Let me stitch up the wound."

Jeremy extended his arm and I took the gauze off. Blood was dripping and pus was

forming around the wounds. I poured rubbing alcohol over the cuts and began stitching up

Jeremy's lacerations. Jeremy screamed, "Oh Dear God, Lord Jesus", as I inserted and completed

the first stitch.

Jeremy pushed me away from him and drunk a swig of the rubbing alcohol. "For the

pain."

I slapped the bottle out of his hand. "Are you crazy? That's poisonous. Stop acting like a

baby and let me finish."

Jeremy hopped out the car and opened the trunk. I saw him hack at Professor James' body

through the opening in the trunk door.

After a few minutes, Jeremy returned with Professor James' right hand, dripping blood at the severed wrist. I said, "What's that for?"

"The pain."

Jeremy put the hand in his mouth and extended his arms. I stitched up Jeremy's arm as he grunted and bit down into the professor's hand. You could hear the cracking and crunching of the professor's hand bones with each stitch that I put into Jeremy's arm. I replaced the gauze after I stitched it up.

We drove to campus and parked near the football stadium. I emptied the blue suitcase in my car and walked to the trunk. The parking lot was empty and there was no one in sight. Jeremy and I lifted Professor James' body out of the trunk. We spread it out on the concrete and began cutting off his limbs. It was surprisingly difficult. We twisted the limbs and head all the way around to dislocate them. Next we cut through the flesh that held them to the body. We threw the torso back in the trunk and put the limbs and head into the blue suitcase. We rolled the suitcase through campus until we got to the math department's three story building. A flag pole was posted in the grass in front of the math building, but with no flag on it. We opened the suitcase and placed the professor's head in front of the doors. We placed the professor's left hand and right hand around the rope on the flag pole and squeezed the stiff hands around the rope, tight. We pulled on the rope until the hands rose to the top of the flag pole. We tossed the right arm and left arm on the ground and beat on two windows on the side of the building with the professor's legs until the glass broke. With the bloody legs, we wrote the Washington Bay Vampires' trademark message on the glass doors at the front of the building. We threw a leg through the windows on each side of the glass doors and headed back to the car. Jeremy was looking at his feet the whole time that we walked back. I smiled. "What's wrong? Guilty conscience?"

"You could say that."

"Well. It's j like you said, just imagine the person you are killing is someone that bullied you or is someone that did you wrong."

"Yeah, you're right. So how have things been between you and Lisa?"

"They've been okay, I guess. Why?"

"Just curious. What attracted you to her in the first place?"

"I don't know. She had a great body; she was easy to talk to. She was the first girl in a long time to treat me like a dateable guy. She never treated me like I was a creep."

"Oh. I see."

"Why don't you give her a call and see what she's been up to? Just because she and I are talking doesn't mean that you can't be friends with her."

"Maybe tomorrow sometime. Hey, I know the perfect place to dump the professor's torso. Let me show you."

We popped the trunk and carried the professor's torso to the gate surrounding the football field. With it, we climbed the fence. We carried the torso to the center of the field and dropped it in the grass. Jeremy turned around, walked a feet few and knelt down, looking at the ground. I smiled. "Can't do it anymore? Just a few more murders and it will be like it was before you were arrested."

I knelt down in front of Jeremy. I placed my hand on his shoulder. "Speak your mind. President Mitchell is the only one left that we have to kill and then it's show time. Finally time for our identities to be revealed to the media. We're going to be big, I can see."

I lost my train of thought as a familiar voice behind me said, "It's been a while, Greg."

Tears ran down my face and I turned around, slurring, "Richard!"

Richard came towards me out of the shadows. "Back from the dead."

#

Fourteen

I shook my head. "I must be hallucinating, or outta my mind. This can't be real."

Richard grinned. "No. It's not a dream. I'm not a mirage. I'm alive."

I brushed my hair with my hands. "How? I saw you die. It was in the newspapers. Jeremy, what is going on?"

Jeremy said in a monotone voice, "Did you ever hear of Richard's funeral? Did you ever get an invite? Did you ever recheck the papers? The newspapers are always trying to get the story first. Sometimes they use the best information that they have available at that time."

Richard said, "I left the hospital early against the doctor's advice. When the reporters came to interview me and saw that I was missing, they tried to ask the staff about my whereabouts and my condition. The staff was not able to clarify any information about me, because of the Hippocratic laws against talking about patients, so the reporters assumed that I was dead. If you checked the papers a few days later, you will notice that they posted the same story with updated information. They described the incident as two stabbings done by the Washington Bay Vampires, instead of a murder and a stabbing."

I wiped the tears from my eyes. "Richard. You don't know how much that I have missed you. This is a dream come true. The crew is back together, just like old times. For a minute there, with Jeremy locked up and you dead, I thought that I would have to start a new life alone, grieving over the both of you. What good is money if there is no one to share it with, and what's a new life with no old friends to grow with?"

I stood up and started walking towards Richard with arms wide. Richard pulled out a gun and aimed it at me. I put my hands up. "Richard. What is this?"

Richard shakes his head. "You've gone too far, Greg. First it was selling t-shirts that said *I am a Washington Bay Vampire* and then you go around breaking our rules of no personal murders. You killed Blondie. You killed two innocent girls. Plus Eric. Jake. All of them. People that had nothing to do with our plans."

I sternly said, "I was trying to pay back Larry for killing you, and without him to give evidence the police would have to free Jeremy. I did it for you."

Richard shook his head. "You did for you. If you really did for us, you would have listened to Jeremy when he said don't ruin our plans to get Blondie. He told you that he had a lawyer and that he would fight the case on his own, but you had to take things into your own hands.

Richard frowned, "Now the police are going to make the connection between the deaths of Eric, Blondie and Jake. As a result, they are going to find out your role in Sarah's murder and they are going to find out your plot to silence Blondie. All of your actions in their eyes will be premeditated. You're going to ruin our chances to get off scot-free. And I don't plan to on spending the rest of my life in jail, or getting the death penalty. So there are only two ways out of this. We can go back to our regular lives, forget all the murders, and give up on our dreams, or we can kill you and play you off as a copycat who imitated our murders."

My eyes started to water. "Richard. It's me. Greg. I've been your best friends since high school. Who you going to hang with, when you start your new life? Who can you trust to have your back and support you, especially when the media and the general public are calling you a monster for these murders? It'll help to have a partner in crime.

I opened my arms wide, "Okay. Listen. I'll disappear and you guys won't ever hear about me again. I'll act like I don't even know you guys. Come on, Richard. Jeremy. Look at me. We're brothers. We planned this together and I've done most of the work. While you were gone, I pushed myself to care of our business. Our business. I felt ashamed about being so weak for the victims. I felt like I was letting you guys down and I pushed myself to overcome parts of my humanity to honor our pack and what the Washington Bay Vampires represent. Jeremy, look at me!"

Jeremy got up and walked over next to Richard. He turned around, looked at me and pulled a pistol from his pocket. Even as he aimed the pistol at my head, Jeremy wiped a tear from his eye. "Sorry, Greg, but you didn't listen and I told you."

I shouted, "Fuck you, Jeremy."

Jeremy shook his head, "Why couldn't you listen to my advice? All you had to do was leave my case alone and take care of our plans. My head feels like crap."

Richard pulled the hammer on his gun and Jeremy wobbled to the side as he pulled the hammer on his own. "Everything is so blurry. I think I'm starting to see stars."

Richard said, "Maybe you should sit down in the grass until I finish off Greg."

Jeremy collapsed on his knees in front of Richard. "My head. Dear Lord."

Richard shouted, "Jeremy! You're bleeding. The back of your shirt is nearly soaked in blood. What happened? Lift up your shirt."

Jeremy took off his shirt. "This girl stabbed me with a pocket knife."

As Richard looked over Jeremy's wound, I took off running towards the bleachers. I heard several gun shots behind me. I turned and saw Jeremy laying in the grass and Richard running after me. I ran up the bleachers and down through a staircase in the middle of the seats. The staircase led to the footballs field's gates. I heard two more shots behind me as I began to climb the fence. I hopped down and yelled loudly as a bullet ricochet off my right shoulder, cutting me. I ran to car and jumped in. Richard yelled, "Take it like a man Greg, stop running!" A bullet struck my cracked windshield, collapsing it.

I sped ahead towards Richard as he shot at me. A bullet hit me in the right cheek, and came out of my left cheek. I felt a wash of pain in my mouth as I grabbed my jaw and as my vision got blurry. I hit my head on the steering wheel as the car crashed into something or someone. The car crash knocked me unconscious for a few seconds. I lifted my head to see what I had run over.

When I came to, I crawled out of the car, held my cheeks for a second and spit a loose tooth out. I took off running across campus. I stopped at the Paddy Foot dorm and walked inside. The resident assistant was doing paper work at her desk. "What happened to you? You look horrible."

I slurred, "I got in a car accident. Can I use the phone to call a cab?"

"Sure. You need me to call an ambulance?"

"No, thanks. I'll be alright."

I called a cab and had the driver take me to my parents' place.

It was around five o' clock in the morning, when I arrived home. I banged on the door for several minutes before my mom opened the door. "Oh, Greg. What happened to you face?"

"I got in an accident. I wrecked the car"

"Open your mouth. Did you lose a tooth?"

"I hit my mouth on the steering wheel. Can I sleep here for a while? Someone broke into my apartment yesterday and I don't feel safe there."

"Of course, baby. We need to get you to hospital to stitch up your mouth first. Let me throw something on and take you."

My mom got dressed and drove me to the urgent care to stitch up my mouth and gums. On the way, she asked, "Is your car repairable? Where did you crash?"

"Near the school stadium. I was visiting a friend last night. I fell asleep at the wheel and I ran into a light pole. The car is completely ruined."

"Baby, if you were tired you should have stayed home or pulled over to the side of the road and got some rest. Did you get a ticket?"

"No. The police said that the school would probably talk to me about the incident on Monday, when Thanksgiving break is over."

We arrived at the urgent care and went in to get me treated.

A few hours later, we drove back to my parent's house. I fell asleep on the couch for a few hours. When I woke up, my mother was up in her bedroom sleeping and I could hear my father outside working on his car. It was little after noon. The news was covering Larry's death at the park and then a breaking report interrupted the coverage. The reporter said that the police had found Professor James dead on campus, his body chopped up into pieces and scattered around the building for the math department. The police said that evidence found on the scene led them to believe that the killing of Professor James was connected to the Washington Bay Vampire killings. The most ground breaking part of the story was that the police believed that they have found a suspect in the Washington Bay Vampire killings. The police believed that Richard Walters is the Washington Bay Vampire or one of the Washington Bay Vampires. The police were unsure if Richard worked with anyone else in the killings. The report went on to say that Richard was found dead next to the stadium where Professor James' body was found. The police found Richard on top of the hood of a car that crashed into the ticket booth at the entrance of the stadium. The front windshield was shattered completely and police recovered a blue suitcase containing two Washington Bay Vampire costumes and several bloody weapons. The police believe that Richard killed Professor James and crashed his car while trying to speed away before anyone saw him, leaving the scene. The police believed that Richard died on impact.

The news flashed a clip of a police conference that took place earlier this morning. The police chief said that he was glad to tell the people of Miami-Dade and Fort Lauderdale city that the police have found the Washington Bay Vampire and they are now looking over evidence to find out if there were any other suspects involved in the killings. The chief went on to say that if they found out there were additional suspects involved, the police would aggressively follow all leads and evidence to capture them. The chief was glad to tell the public that the Washington Bay killings may have been brought to an end and that hopefully some of the families that were victimized will be given some kind of closure. The police chief ended by saying, "Now that the Vampires' reign of terror is over, we can all sleep a little bit more peacefully at night and walk a little bit more securely in the daytime."

I turned off the television and went in the kitchen to get something to eat. My dad walked into the house and sat down to eat lunch with me. I asked my dad if I could crash at home until school started back up on Monday and he nodded.

#

A few days had passed and on Sunday, I asked my mom to drive me back to my apartment.

Before entering, I checked my mail and looked around the outside of my apartment building for any signs of a break in. All the windows looked secured and good as new. My front door didn't have any cracks in it or around the frame. I entered my house and grabbed a knife out of my kitchen. I walked throughout my apartment, looking in all the areas that made good hiding spaces. No one was hiding in my apartment. I changed into something comfortable and began

watching South Park. My cell phone rang from an unknown number calling me. I picked up.

"Who is this?"

"This is detective Ryan Ronald from the Fort Lauderdale police department. How are

you? This is Greg Rotten, right?"

"Yes. What do you need?"

"I know that you're busy at the moment, but I need to ask you about your Nissan. You

own a red Nissan right?"

"Correct."

"We found your car crashed into the ticket booth near the Washington Bay stadium"

"What! How did it get there?"

"Apparently, someone—do you know Richard Walters?"

"Yeah. I know of him."

"Richard crashed your car into the ticket booth a few days ago and died in the crash. I'm

sorry to tell you."

"My goodness. That's awful. I let him borrow my car for the week. I feel so sorry for his

family."

"You let him borrow your car for the week? So you guys are friends?"

"Something like that. We hung out a few times. We went to high school together, but we

were more like acquaintances then. I hung out with him a few times at his dorm room and he

asked me to use my car to visit some girl in the Florida Keys for Thanksgiving break. I let him

borrow my car in exchange for him to write my five-thousand word English essay for me."

"What day did you lend him the car?"

"On Monday. Sometime in the afternoon."

"Did you see him at all after you gave him the car?"

"I haven't seen him since. No one called me to tell me he was dead. Or anything like that. This is a lot for me to process right now. First an acquaintance of mine dies in a car accident and, to add to that, I'm out of car."

"I'm sorry to break the bad news to you, but I needed to find out how Richard got a hold of your car and if you have information regarding the death of Professor James. Did Richard ever mention his feelings to you about Professor James? Did he say anything about hurting Professor James or about hurting anyone?"

"Richard never said anything bad about anyone. He was very mild mannered and quiet, most of the time."

"On Monday, did Richard seem stressed or worried at all?"

"He seemed very calm, to me at least. I didn't really know him well enough to tell when he was not his usual self."

"If you have any information about the murder of Professor James or if anything comes to mind that you feel that I need to know about Richard, please give me a call."

"Definitely. Thank you, bye."

I hung up the phone and grabbed a beer out of the fridge. I sat down on the couch and guzzled down the beer. I turned the channel found Scarface playing on the H. B. O. channel. There was a scene in the movie where Tony Montana nearly drowns his face in a pile of cocaine. The stress of living an ungodly life with a guilty conscience, in the pursuit of material things, weighs heavily upon him. What good was pursuing material things the fast way, if you had to stress about how to outsmart the police or check around the outside of your apartment to see if someone broke in your house to kill you? All of this while trying to be a pharmacy student. I was

failing my classes because I couldn't concentrate. When I wasn't daydreaming about life after my

book deal, my mind was plagued with flashbacks of killing Mrs. Sternverger, Rachel, Eric, Jake,

and Larry.   At times the flashbacks would be pleasurable. I felt good to stand up to society

and pay it back for all the emotional and psychological abuse that I had received just because I

wasn't popular or the norm. At other times, the flashbacks stressed me out, confused me, made

me feel guilty and scared me. Reevaluating my motives for partaking in the murders, it was

starting to seem like I committed all of them in vain. Who was to say that my book would be a

success? For all I know, this murder spree might cause me to face a lot of shame and scorn

because of the killings, with no benefit at all. There were times I wondered, why did killing

popular people make me feel good, anyway? Was it because I was jealous of them? Did I feel if I

wasn't happy, then no one else was going to be happy, either? I often overcame these thoughts by

reminding myself it was the popular kids who bullied me and made me feel worthless. A plain

existence wouldn't even be that bad if you had support and respect from your peers. In high

school, most of my popular peers tormented me with nonstop teasing that turned into years of

emotional abuse. It's no wonder I had so much anger built up in me. I didn't envy my popular

peers; I hated them and wanted the torture to end. I wanted to live my life without being judged.

I wanted to be respected as a person by everyone. This murder spree seemed like a stepping

stone to a place where maybe I could find some respect and peace. I often daydreamed about

living on a foreign island and socializing with polite and friendly natives. However, the news

coverage on the murders started to raise doubts that my day dreams would ever happen. All these

interviews with the families of the victims were raising up the fear that I would be paid back for

these crimes. Since the time I had killed Mrs. Sternverger, I had tossed and turned in bed almost every night. My friend had gotten locked up and then my friends tried to kill me. My guilty

conscience would sit heavily on my heart every time I saw a black girl with braids. I had already

begun to be punished for my crimes. The stress on my mind and heart had to end.

Scarface was coming to a close and was at my favorite scene. A drug lord sends his gang

members to Tony Montana's house to kill him. Tony doesn't cower at the sight of his enemies;

instead he takes it like a man and has a shootout. Tony dies as a result of the shootout, but took

out nearly all of his adversaries. Although Tony died, I'm sure the drug lord will never forget his

name after finding out how many of his associates he lost trying to kill Tony. Tony had the right

idea when it came to dealing with stress. When your back is against the wall, bring the pain.

Fight with everything you have and never let them see you in need. Pressure sometimes pushes

people to do things that they never knew they were capable of.

I knew just what to do. I turned off the television and took the bus to Wal-Mart.

I bought a black, twin size bed sheet, a pair of stockings, a hunting knife and a meat fork.

When I got home, I made a gown and mask out of the black bed sheet and one of the stockings. I

put the vampire outfit, the hunting knife, and the meat fork in my book bag. I took a hot bath to

calm my nerves, before I worked on my homework. After a few hours of studying, I went to bed.

#

Fifteen

The next morning, I woke up in time to catch the bus to campus. I walked to the financial

aid building and walked up to the office of the school's president. There was a secretary sitting at a desk near the entrance. I asked, "Is it possible that I could schedule an appointment with the president today? I really need to speak with President Mitchell. I'm unsure if I will have the money to attend school next semester. Someone told me that I could possibly talk to the president to see if he could help me get some scholarship money or waive my tuition for next semester."

"The president is having a meeting with another student right now.. He has a meeting with the staff in an hour. I don't think that he will be able to see you today you can schedule an appointment with the vice president, I'm sure that he can assist you with your concerns."

"No, thanks. The president's office is in this room?"

"It's upstairs, but you can't walk into his office without an appointment. You can schedule an appointment for tomorrow, if you like."

"Tomorrow I'm busy. So I'll try again later this week."

I left the office and headed to the elevator. I went up to the top floor, the fourth story. The president's office and a large conference room were the only two rooms on the whole floor. There was no one walking in the hall on the fourth. I walked down to the president's office and placed my ear on the door. I didn't hear anyone in the room. The president's door was made of solid wood. There was a peephole on the door but no windows on or near it. I walked to the conference room on the other end of the hall. I walked in and shut the door behind me. There was nothing in the e room except a long table and lots of chairs. I opened my book bag and took out my vampire outfit. I dressed and put the hunting knife and meat fork in my pocket. I stuck my ear to the door to listen for anyone walking in the hallway. Nothing. I opened the door and slowly walked down towards the president's office. I took out the hunting knife, knocked on the president's door and waited a minute. No one answered the door. I wiggled the door knob and found it unlocked. So I opened the door and walked into the President's office. The office was large and made an L shape. The office had to be about thirty feet long from the wall near the book case to the wall, parallel to it, across the room. There was a desk sitting three feet across from the front door with a tall bookcase next to it. The office had navy blue carpeting.. There was a round table and a couch several feet to the right of the desk. I walked around the desk and looked under it. I walked over to the red couch, climbed on top of it and looked behind it. I heard a familiar voice to my right say, "I figured that you'd come here."

I stepped back off the couch and looked to my right. "Jeremy!"

There was a wooden rectangular table with chairs near the end of the office. A private bathroom was to the left of the table and a counter with a sink was built into the wall. Some guy and president Mitchell were lying across the wooden table with blood all over them and with pieces of their intestines hanging out of their stomachs. Blood was dripping from the two front corners of the table. Jeremy was sitting on the counter, cutting pieces of the intestines into pieces. One the wall to my right was our signature message written in blood. I walked towards the table. "I thought that rubbing alcohol killed you. You nearly passed out on the field."

"I passed out for a few seconds and the next thing I know I hear police sirens in the far distance. Richard left me, so I took off before the police found me at the scene. It sucks. Betrayed by both of my friends."

"Richard is dead. You don't watch the news?"

"That explains a lot. No, I've been sleeping and hiding out in Richard's car since the last time I saw you. I didn't know if the police were looking for me."

"Why did you want to kill me, Jeremy? Are you angry about Lisa? Were you jealous?"

"Why did you have to take Lisa from me? You knew I liked that girl."

"You told me that you were okay with it. If I had known that you were going to get this worked up about her, I would have never even talked to her."

"But you did and you don't even feel guilty about doing it. Some friend. You can kill people for me, but you can't kill your attraction to the girl that I'm in love with."

"I'm sorry. You can have her back. If it means anything to you, I haven't spoken to her in at least a week and we have never even went on one date. I'm not even sure that she is still interested in me."

Jeremy pulls a gun from his pocket. "I should kill you for this."

I put up my hands. "Jeremy. You are going to need a friend to start your new life with. What good is fame and money, if you don't have anyone to share it with or anyone that truly cares about you? We're brothers. President Mitchell is dead. His death was the last part of our plan. The only thing left for us to do is to get caught in the act and hope that we get a good book and movie deal. If you kill me, you are going to be under tons of stress going through the media circus by yourself. It'll help to have someone to endure the stress with you."

"I thought about that and I thought about a way that you can make it up to me."

"Whatever it takes."

Jeremy hopped off the counter and opened the bathroom door. Jeremy pulled Lisa, gagged and tied up, out of the bathroom by her feet. Jeremy laid her next to President Mitchell. "Kill her. Show me that you really are my brother."

"No personal murders, remember?"

"Kill her. More than likely, no one has ever seen you two together."

Jeremy held the gun by the nose. "Take it. If you don't, you are no longer my brother. I'll give you a minute to think about it."

I took off my mask and gown and tossed them on the floor. "Remember, we're supposed to kill in a way that makes it seem like we're insane without *becoming* insane. I can't kill someone that is innocent."

"Weren't Jake and Eric innocent? What about Rachel?"

"What about them? They associated with the type of people that alienated me, but Lisa has been a friend to both you and me."

"What a joke! Lisa is a friend to no one; she stood both of us up. The girl cares for no one but herself, lousy tramp. Do us both a favor, Greg, and kill the dumb broad."

A few moments of silence went by. Jeremy shook his hea., "I see you've made your choice."

Jeremy walked over to Lisa and put the gun to her head. "Thanks for being such a great pal, stupid bitch."

He pulled the trigger four times. Jeremy aimed the gun at me. "One part of me wants to kill you, Greg, and another part wants to let you go, but for the wrong that you have done me, retaliation is a must. I considered earlier the possibility that you wouldn't be able to kill Lisa, so this is how we can make things right between me and you. I'm going to turn myself in as the one and only mastermind of the Washington Bay Vampire killings. You will not take any credit for the murders and state that you had no involvement in the killings. You will tell the media and the police that I confessed all the killings to you over these past few weeks. You will tell the police in detail how I killed the victims. You will tell creepy stories about me to the police and media that make me seem dark and scary. I will write a book and you will support all the claims that I make, however, you will not share in any of the profits. I will start a new life without you."

"You can't do this to me. I've worked just as hard as you have, carrying out and planning the murders. Give me some other way."

"I gave you a way to make it right and it turns out that you have a pink belly."

I shouted, "I don't have to listen to you. You're going to kill me, Jeremy. Go ahead. Now that I'm out of a new life and a book deal, I don't have much to look forward to," as I gave Jeremy the finger.

"No, I'm not going to kill you. You betrayed me and I want you to pay. Death is the easy way out for you. I would rather you see me on television, living it up in the spotlight."

"I'm going to turn myself in also."

"You do that and I'll tell the police that you killed Eric, Jake and Larry in order to set me free from jail. Those murders have a logical motive and it will be hard for you to get off on an insanity plea. Even if you get a book deal, you'll never be able to enjoy it, behind bars with a life sentence. You might even get the death penalty."

"You monster."

Suddenly, sirens could be heard outside the window. Jeremy smiled and grabbed my mask and gown. "Toss me your knife and meat fork."

I tossed Jeremy the fork and hunting knife. Jeremy aimed the gun at my leg. "When they ask you, tell the police that you, Lisa, and Ralph, on the table, had an appointment with President Mitchell. I busted into the room told you guys to get on the ground and then I stabbed Ralph in the back. You tried to run and I shot you in the leg. You watched in horror as I killed President Mitchell, Lisa and Ralph."

"I got it. Shot in the leg?"

Jeremy shot me in the leg and I fell to the floor. "Jesus!"

The police kicked the door open and ran into the room. The officers shouted, "Put the weapon down and get on the floor!"

Jeremy dropped his gun and knelt down on the floor. The police arrested Jeremy and the paramedics took me to the ambulance on a stretcher.

I arrived at the hospital and immediately went through surgery to repair the wound on my leg.

A few hours after surgery, a police officer entered my room and asked what happened in the president's office. I told him that Jeremy had come into the office with a gun and executed President Mitchell, Ralph, and Lisa in front of me, and then Jeremy shot me in the leg as I tried to run away to safety. The police asked me to come into the station to give them a written statement. I agreed to give the statement, once I left the hospital.

My mom came to visit me, as soon as she received the news, today, that I was in the hospital. My mom approached my bed, "Jesus. What in the world happened to you, Greg?"

I took a deep breath. "One of my best friends tried to kill me."

"I'm so glad that you are okay. I was scared to death, when I found out that you were in surgery. I took off work for the day and I'm going to stay here with you for the rest of the day. I'll be back every day until you recover."

My mother wiped a tear from her eye, "Sweetie, what happened?"

"I was going to see President Mitchell to ask him about if there was any kind of scholarship available, next semester that help me with the tuition. My friend Lisa said that she also was curious about the availability of scholarships for next semester as well and walked with me to the President's office. All of a sudden, while Lisa and I are talking with the President, Jeremy came out of nowhere with a gun and killed Lisa and the president. Jeremy shot me in the leg as I tried to run away. He then attempted to kill me as well, but the cops interrupted his attempt on my life."

My mother hugged me and kissed my forehead, "That's horrible! What is this world coming too! Where did you meet Jeremy?"

"I've known Jeremy since High School. He just never came over, because he lives about an hour from where we stay."

"Did the police catch Jeremy?"

"Yeah, he's in the county jail right now, with no bail."

"I almost had a heart attack when I found out that you got shot, while I was at work. The police had contacted me and told me that you were in the hospital. I rushed here to make sure that you were alright. I found out about your friend Richard. I feel so bad for you, Greg. This is the second time that someone tried to kill you and on top of that, one of your best friends died. I'm so sorry, Greg."

"I'll be alright."

"Do you want me to get you anything from the store while you're here?"

"No, thanks. Can you please turn on the news for me?"

My mom picked up the remote control and turned to the news on channel seven. The news was covering a special break on the murders of President Mitchell and two students on Washington Bay campus. The reporter went on to say that one person was injured during the murder spree and recovering at the hospital. The police had a suspect in custody and believed that suspect, Jeremy Winters, was an accomplice in the Washington Bay Vampire killings. A picture of Jeremy flashed on the screen as they continued talking about the murders and Jeremy's past. The police found evidence on the scene that linked the Washington Bay Vampire Killings to the murders of President Mitchell, Ralph Beard, and Lisa Montez. The reporter added that Jeremy had recently come under suspicion of killing Sarah Reynolds, but was set free because of lack of evidence. My mom handed me the remote and I flicked the channel to channel five, which was covering the same story. While discussing Jeremy's past, it brought up his history of violence in high school and his evaluations by a child psychologist that he visited in the past.

A few hours later, I left the hospital against the doctor's advice and took a taxi to the police station. I sat down with a few officers and told them a detailed account of how Jeremy busted into President Mitchell's office and killed President Mitchell, Ralph, and Lisa.

One of the officers asked, "Did you know Jeremy well?"

"I've known Jeremy since high school. We were close friends and shared some of our deepest and darkest secrets with one another. He told me a while back that he had killed Mrs. Sternverger, Melvin Peters, sixteen sorority girls on a bus and some girl that lived in the Paddy Foot dorm. Jeremy told me that Richard assisted him in the murders and that Richard told him that he killed Larry, Rachel, Jake, Eric, two girls that lived near Jake and Eric, sixteen sorority girls on a party bus and a man that lived on the same floor. I had always been creeped out by Jeremy and Richard. I don't even know why I hung out with them. I remember once, Jeremy showed me a clip on his computer of him torturing and killing a cat. It made me want to vomit. I think that Jeremy and Richard were psychopaths. Jeremy showed me some of the weapons that he had used in the murders with the blood still on them. I couldn't sleep that night. Richard and Jeremy threatened to kill me if I talked to you guys. But now that Richard is dead and Jeremy is in custody, I feel a little bit safer and a little less stressed. Now I can get this off my chest and share all this information with you."

"Are you willing to put all that you have told us in writing and testify in court to this information, if we request your assistance?"

"Off course. I just want to bring closure to the families."

I gave the police a written statement of everything that I had told them. I circled Jeremy's picture out of a line up, identifying him as the one who had shot me. The police dropped me off at my parents' house and I sat on the couch to watch the news.

#

Sixteen

The next day, one of the news channels was showing an interview that they had with Jeremy. A blond male reporter asked Jeremy about his past and how he grew up.

The reporter asked Jeremy if he had suffered any sexual of physical abuse as a child.

Jeremy replied, "No, my parents were wonderful to me. I did, however, experience a lot of bullying in high school. I was a loner and most people considered me strange because I didn't want to kiss their behinds to fit in."

The reporter went on to ask Jeremy why he killed his victims.

Jeremy replied, "I was setting their souls free. My victims were bullied on campus, just like me. I was setting them free. When a vampire bites you, your body and soul is transformed. You are no longer the prey but the predator. You become immortal and can do whatever you like. However, food and water will not be enough to sustain a visible earthy presence. You need to feed on the blood of people to maintain yourself; otherwise you will disappear into the shadows of the night and never be seen again."

A few moments of dead silence passed. The reporter shook his head. "Okay. So you were trying to help your victims. I see now."

Next he asked Jeremy about his life on Washington Bay campus. Jeremy told the reporter that he hung out with Richard and I. Jeremy informed the reporter that he had confessed the murders to me and threatened to kill me, if I had told anyone.

The interview lasted a couple hours. A few hours later, I got a phone call from a writer named Sharon Sanchious. Sharon Sanchious is a journalist for a newspaper in Miami called the Sunshine Times. Sharon is also a published author that writes true crime stories. She has written five best sellers and owns a publishing company. Ms. Sanchious has helped many victims of crime, criminals, crime accomplices and many jurors write down and turn their experiences, stories, feelings and thoughts into successful novels and successful biographies. Sharon asked me if I was interested in helping her write a book on the Washington Bay Killings by providing her with firsthand experience of what it was like hanging out with Jeremy and Richard. I told her that I wasn't interested for personal reasons.

#

A few months later, Jeremy's trial began. Jeremy had pleaded not guilty by reason of insanity and his lawyer began arguing in his favor. The newspapers came down hard on Jeremy, calling him a monster and a freak. The newspapers talked about the police finding video clips of Jeremy torturing animals and how the school did a poor job in neglecting to see the warning signs that Jeremy gave off. The newscaster reported that Jeremy had received several death threats while in prison. The anchorman announced that someone had set fire to the dorm room that Jeremy stayed in after hearing on the news that Jeremy got a book deal for three million dollars. The newsreader reported that the book Jeremy was writing was called *The Murder Spree of a Real Life Vampire*. The news also reported that Jeremy's mom visited him often, but his dad refused to see him.

During the first day of trial, angry protestors carried posters outside the courthouse and showed cartoon pictures of Jeremy being brutally murdered. The protestors also wore t-shirts with pictures of the victims on them. The t-shirts had sayings embroidered on the back. Some read: *Remembering the victims, I can't stomach Jeremy Winters, Don't support the book The Murder Spree of a Real Life Vampire* and *Jeremy Winters deserves the death penalty.*

A week into Jeremy's trial, I turned on the television and my mouth dropped. It can't be. At the bottom of the screen, it read: *Jeremey Winters, The Washington Bay Vampire, Dead.*

page 206 of 212

I shook my head as the newscaster said, "Jeremy Winters, also known as the Washington Bay Vampire was killed today in the Florenda minimum security jail facility, today. Jeremy's father, Alex Winters, met Jeremy in the visitor room for the inmates. During an argument, they got into a physical fight. Jeremy's father put Jeremy in a sleeper hold and snapped his neck before security could get to them. He was arrested and charged with manslaughter.

When I heard the news report on Jeremy's death a day later, I turned off the television and threw the remote control at the wall, "Damn. Jeremy."

I shed a tear and picked up the phone to call Sharon Sanchious. Richard and Jeremy would have wanted at least one of us to share in the fruits of our labor. After all the abuse that we had suffered from society, we deserved a better life. Since Richard and Jeremy are no longer with me, I'll just have to live it up for them. I dialed Sharon's number.

Sharon answered the phone, "This is Sharon."

"Hi. It's Greg. I was calling to take up that offer to work with you on putting together a book on the Washington Bay murders. I think that it will be great therapy for me to share my thoughts and experiences about all the events that surrounded the murders."

"Well, I'm glad that you are still interested and that you kept me in your thoughts. There are a lot of people that have been watching the Jeremy Winters trial and are looking for lots of answers to all the questions that they have about Jeremy Winters and the killing spree that took place on campus. The coverage on Jeremy's trial was nationwide. It is the top story covered on nearly every news station. I think that a collection of your accounts with Jeremy and Richard can help bring closure to the families that suffered as a result of the homicides that occurred on campus."

"Great! Maybe we can meet up, sometime this week and make an outline for the book. Do you really think that a book on the Washington Bay Vampires will sell?"

"Of Course! I've help many criminals, victims, and associates of criminals and victims put together books that sold over 100 thousand copies in two months. Do you remember the machete chef that killed many of his coworkers, chopped up their bodies and cooked them as delicacies that he served to over 100 guests?"

"Oh yeah! I remember that guy. He got sentenced to death by lethal injection last year, if I remember correctly."

"I visited him in jail and helped him put together a 300 page autobiography on his life and his killings. His book has sold over 500, 000 copies. Unfortunately, most of his money has gone to the families of his victims. As they should. He shouldn't be able to benefit off someone else' suffering. But in your case it's different. You are just an innocent bystander who witnessed, first hand, the growth of a monster and has been traumatized by the whole ordeal. In addition to all this. You are the only who can give us a true account of what Jeremy and Richard were like and what their plans were on campus. You can give the trail spectators and the families of the victims the answers they are looking for. I think that after all that you have suffered, you deserved the monetary benefits that come from writing this book. I see it as a form of reparation for all the grief and pain that you have suffered as the result of being tormented by what you hear and knew Richard and Jeremy did, and losing two close friends."

"I appreciate your concern and this opportunity."

"Yes lets meet on Saturday around noon. Is that a good time for you?"

"Yes, that sounds perfect. I'm free on Saturday."

"Awesome! I'll see you Saturday. We'll put together a first draft outline."

"Nice Talking to you. Good Bye!"

I hung up the phone and slouched back against the couch. Now that Jeremy was dead, I would paint an even darker view of Jeremy as a sociopath who killed for attention and admired monsters like Charles Manson. I would tell the world how Jeremy wanted to become America's Next Top Vampire.

#

It took Sharon and me about three months to finish the book. The book became a best seller. I figured that I would get my degree in the United States and then move away to start a new life.

#

After receiving my funds from my book, my family and I moved to Hawaii. I attended the University of Hawaii, changed my major from pharmacy to English and got a Bachelor's degree.

After graduation, I moved to the Philippines. In my first month there, I met and dated more women than I had dated in my entire life. Although I have a half of a million dollars in my bank account, from the selling of my book, I work as an English teacher in the Philippines. I taught many English classes for adults and became good friends with lots of my students. After several semesters of teaching, I have made many friends. I'm glad to tell you that after a year of dating hot, Asian women, I finally found a woman that is not only beautiful, but shares a lot in common with me. My wife loves the movie *Scarface*. I am now happily married with one kid. Since I landed in the Philippines, I have slept better than I have before the killings. I rarely think of them and have even forgotten the faces of the people that I killed. As a result of my testimony against Jeremy, the prosecutor in Jeremy's case granted me immunity. The police never questioned me as a suspect in any of the murders. The police never connected me to any of the murders. It's as if I never killed anyone and the Washington Bay killings never happened.

The only time that I remember anything is when I think of Richard and Jeremy. To be honest with you, my new life in the Philippines is so soothing that I barely think of Richard and Jeremy. Does that make me a bad friend? Starting a new life is not just about leaving the bad memories behind, but the good memories as well.

www.ingramcontent.com/pod-product-compliance
Lightning Source LLC
Chambersburg PA
CBHW082225140626
46556CB00019B/3228